NO

No Regrets
Book One

Regrets

while, learning how not to be deceived by him, or his lies. My mother, however, not so much.

"Abbygail?" he whispered, noticing the tears rolling down my cheek. "Why are you crying?"

I met his worried dark eyes. "Because I don't have a dad."

"What do you mean? Of course, you have a dad. Everyone has one. It's the only way to make babies."

Snickering at his response, I looked at him sitting beside me. Oliver might have been four months younger than I was, but he was already way taller than me. He had dark hair like mine, and deep chestnut eyes, which were so different from my blue ones. He said my eyes changed color depending on my mood: some days they were crystal blue, and other days they were ocean blue. My mother said I had my father's eyes. I always wondered if she thought it was a good thing or not because every time she spoke about him, it was in a negative way.

"That's not what I mean, Ol. I mean that Simon never comes to see me. It's like he doesn't want to be my dad anymore."

"Well, if you ask me, your dad's a jerk. I'm going to ask my dad if he can be your dad too."

I smiled thankful that I had a friend like him in my life. I loved Henry, Oliver's dad, he always took care of me in ways my own father never did.

"Here." He pulled a flower blossom from behind his

back and placed it delicately inside the palm of my hand. "I took it from my mother's plant inside the house. It reminded me of your eyes."

"What is it?" I traced the lines of the various shades of deep blue ridges that covered the beautiful white blossom with my eyes.

"A flower."

"Duh! I mean what's it called?"

"I think it's an orchid. "

"An orchid?" I laughed.

"That's what I heard my dad calling it when he gave it to my mom."

"Well, it sounds like a pretty weird name for a flower to me. You must have heard him wrong."

He shrugged.

"It's really beautiful, though."

"It is," he admitted with a shy smile. "Just like you,"

"Eww!"

"What?"

"Don't tell me I'm beautiful."

"Why not?"

"I don't know. It's just weird."

He rolled his eyes. "Fine then. I think you're super ugly."

"Hey!"

"What now?"

"Well, you can't tell a girl she's super ugly,

especially not on her birthday," I pouted. "It's kind of mean."

"But you just—"

"There is such a thing as an 'in between', you know."

He didn't answer. He just huffed as if he was the most annoyed seven-year-old guy on the planet.

"Maybe that's why I don't have a dad. Maybe he thinks I'm too ugly and so mean that I'm not worth his time anymore." I started to cry all over again.

Oliver put his arms around me, soothing my tears as best as he could. "Abby, you are the nicest girl I know. You are the best friend I've ever had, and I swear I will never leave you. I promise that I will never hurt you."

I looked up to his deep chestnut eyes, they were filled with friendship and promises, and I couldn't help but believe him. From that day forward, I knew that Oliver Langton and I would always be together.

CHAPTER ONE

NINE YEARS LATER

OLIVER

"Abbygail."

"What?" She didn't even look up from her floating air mattress, but I did notice her smirk.

It was cold out, a lot cooler than I had anticipated, but that's what happened in Carrington at the end of August. While it was warm and humid during the day, once the sun went down, so did the heat. Yet, after over forty minutes of incessant begging, I still managed to convince Abby to join me in the pool after dinner. I'd never tell her, but I was freezing just as much as she was. Each time my fingers would graze the parts of her skin that wasn't covered by her pink string bikini, she'd shiver, making me smile. I didn't mind because this was *our* time. School was about to start, and that meant having to share my best friend with everyone else all over again.

I just wasn't ready for that yet.

"Abbygail," I growled. "Could you please stop ignoring my questions?"

"I'm not ignoring your questions, Oliver. I'm choosing not to answer them. There's a huge difference."

A slight grin tugged at the corner of my mouth. Abby always found a way to play with words in order to be right. "Maybe it is time for us to go back to school after all."

"Why?"

"Because I think you're having trouble with your vocabulary," I teased. "Ignoring and choosing not to answer means the same thing, Abs."

"It does not." I leaned in and rested my arms and head on the side of her stomach, making her gasp when the cool pool water touched her skin. "Shit, that's cold."

"It wouldn't be so cold if you'd just come in with me."

"I'm not coming in. I already told you: the water's freezing."

"I'm still waiting, you know." She was trying to maintain a certain level of dryness on the pool float she was laying on, but what she didn't know was how fast she'd find herself at the bottom of the pool if she wouldn't give up the information I inquired.

"You can wait as much as you want, Oliver. I'm not going to answer you."

"Fine then." I flipped the mattress and before she had any time to react, her head was submerged in water. I could hear her scream through the air bubbles and laughed.

"What the hell was that for?" she whined when she resurfaced.

"I asked you a question."

"And you think I'm going to answer you now? I swear you have to be the most irritating friend on earth."

"Best friend," I corrected and she stuck out her tongue.

Summer evenings where I could spend some alone time with Abby were the ones I preferred the most. When I came back from football practice that afternoon, my parents were at Abby's house preparing dinner with Jenna, Abby's mother, and Abby was sitting under the tree talking with Kylie.

Aunt Jen and my mom had been paired up as roommates when they started university. Two strangers that knew absolutely nothing about each other when they first met, and now many years later they acted more like sisters than best friends.

Jenna once told us that even after my mother left to

work in British Colombia, they managed to keep their friendship as strong as if they still lived in the same dorm room. B.C. is where my parents met. They worked for the same research facility in Surrey. He wooed her, they dated, moved in together and got married. A few months after their wedding, my grandmother on my mother's side got very ill, and since Aunt Hailey, my mom's sister, couldn't handle the care on her own anymore, my parents decided to move closer to home and help out with her needs. Unfortunately, she passed away after catching a virus her immune-system was unable to recover from, and not long after her mother's passing, my mom found out she was pregnant with me. I was born four months after Abby.

"Why do you even care anyway?" Abbygail asked, reaching for the pool float I had hidden behind me.

I don't care.

I'm jealous.

She glared at me with her piercing blue eyes, and proud of the rise I'd managed to get out of her, I grinned. I would always get a kick out of getting under Abby's skin. Her attempt at pretending to be mad at me was always entertaining. Knowing Abbygail my entire life meant that I knew how to read her. If I wanted to know how she truly felt, I studied her eyes. It always amazed me how their intensity changed with her mood. When she was mad, they were gray. They'd turn crystal blue if she was sad. Whenever she was happy, they were ocean blue. Or at least I thought it was when she was happy...

"I *don't* care. I just want to know who the mystery guy is. Who knows? Maybe I can help you set up a date."

She rolled her eyes at me. "Forget it. I don't need your help with this."

"Is it Stephan?" I couldn't stop myself from asking. The fact that they had gotten closer over the last few weeks of summer was bugging the crap out of me.

She grimaced.

"Then tell me. I don't get it. Don't you trust me?"

"First of all, this has nothing to do with trust, and that was a private conversation between Kylie and me you listened to Oliver Langton. You don't need to know all my secrets, Ol."

"But I'm your best friend. Best friends confide in each other. And news flash, Abbygail, I *do* know all of your secrets."

"Well, apparently not all of them." She wagged her brows, smiling evilly at me.

Abby started to swim away and by the time I reached her, she had already started to climb up the stairs. "I'm cold and I'm getting out. We're done with this conversation, Oliver."

Like hell we are...

"Abby, wait!" I reached out and circled her body

with my arms, dragging her back down into the pool with me. She laughed as she kept trying to find a way to put my head under water.

This was us, being us.

"Okay guys, it's getting late."

At the sound of my mother's voice, Abby's attention shifted for a fraction of a second and before realizing it, her head was back under water.

"Oliver!" she shrieked. By the time she reached the steps, I was already long gone with both of our towels. "Oliver Langton, give me my towel!"

"You want it, come and get it," I hollered, gunning for the willow tree.

"Uncle Henry?" Abby complained to my father.

"Yes, sweetie?"

"Your son is being a pain in my ass again."

I rolled my eyes. She had the worst habit of sucking up to him and making me look bad in the process. "Really, Abby?"

"What did he do now?" my dad asked, a grin tugging at the corner of his lips.

"Yeah, well, you stole my towel," she whined. "And it's fucking cold, Oliver."

"Abbygail, don't swear," her mother disciplined. "I'm expecting a dollar in the swear jar, young lady."

My best friend shot me a dirty look as she joined me under the tree. "This is your fault, you know."

"What's my fault?"

"I'm a dollar poorer because of you."

"Don't blame your swearing on me. I don't control your mouth." *Oh, but I wish I did...*

She crossed her arms over her chest. "You're paying for that slushy tomorrow, just so you know."

I grinned.

"Monkey Butt, give Abbygail her towel," my father berated

"Yeah, Monkey Butt, give me my towel." My glare dared her to mock me again, but her smirk only grew wider.

Curtesy of Abbigail Evens, I had the worse nickname in the history of mankind. When we were twelve years old my parents took Abby and me on a summer vacation. On one of the days we were at the beach, I had somehow forgotten to put some sunscreen on my face. By the end of the day I looked like an overcooked lobster. The following day we visited the Toronto Zoo and passed by the macaque monkeys. As soon as Abby saw the color of their butts, she exploded into laughter and compared my face to their ugly asses. My dad, who was not too far ahead of us, picked up on my aggravation towards my best friend, and for some reason, he thought it would be funny to add fuel to my anger. He went on telling me to get over it and to stop acting like a monkey's butt. Ever since then, both made a point teasing me with it every time they could.

"I agree with your mom, sweetheart," my mother added popping out from inside the house. "It's not pretty for a beautiful young lady like you to swear like you do."

"I'm sorry, Aunt Evelynn."

I snorted. "You're such a suck up."

Abby threw me a side-smirk. "You're just jealous that she likes me better than she likes you."

"Whatever," I replied, rolling my eyes. "So, about that guy—"

"Drop it, Oliver."

"Monkey Butt," my dad called out a second time. "Let's go!"

"Yeah, Monkey Butt." Abby eyed the towel wrapped around my hips and then the one I was holding in my hands. "Besides, I need to get ready too. You know; beauty sleep and all."

"Why?" I placed her pink towel over her shoulders and gave it a light tug. "Who do you need to impress?"

One look at her beautiful face and my jealousy had finally won over my sense of reason. Without thinking through all the possible consequences of my stupidity, I put my lips to hers. They were soft and sweet, tasting better than I would have ever imagined.

Fucking perfection.

I pulled away before she had any time to react and made sure to hide everything I was feeling from her. Pushing away the branches of the willow tree in order to clear myself a passage, I snuck a quick glimpse behind me. The tip of her fingers grazed her lips. She looked stunned and I wasn't sure if that was a good or a bad thing.

There wasn't much I could do to render Abbygail Evens speechless, but that definitely did the trick. In that moment I tried to see her eyes; the need to know how she felt was overwhelming. Unfortunately, it was getting dark, and I couldn't tell what shade of blue I was looking at.

"'Night, Beautiful." My comment pulled her out of her daze, and she regarded me with what seemed like a thousand questions. Instead of answering any of them, I gave her my most charming grin and winked.

ABBYGAIL

Um...

"Abbygail?"

Um... what just happened?

Wait. Did he just wink?

"Abbygail," my mother called out a second time.

I rubbed my temples. I needed some quiet time to think. "What?"

"Aren't you going to say goodnight?"

"Oliver and I already said goodnight, Mom."

"We did not," he replied.

"Shut up, Oliver!"

"Abbygail, don't be mean. And I was talking about you saying goodnight to Evelynn and Henry."

I winced. Of course, she did. I didn't want to walk over there. If Oliver saw my face, then he'd find out how his kiss had affected me. The truth? Not only did I not mind kissing him, but I wanted to—all the time. He, on the other hand, had been doing everything to provoke me for weeks, pushing my buttons repeatedly until I lashed out at him.

Oliver Langton was the one stable point of my life. My rock. We were neighbors, best friends, we went to the same school, we were in the same grade, we shared the same group of friends.

We did everything together.

Well... pretty much everything.

He played football; not my thing. I hated team sports or anything that involved a ball. He skateboarded: it was his passion, which was again not my thing, but we would spend way too many hours at the skate park two blocks down from our houses, and I never got bored watching him. I mostly used that time to admire him from the bleachers while he showed off his skills. Life had deprived me of the coordination I needed to even try to ride a board, and it wasn't from lack of effort. I couldn't count the number of times Oliver had convinced me to let him teach me, and that summer was no different. Last month I sprained my ankle and told him that if he made me do it again I wouldn't talk to him for a month. The concept was absolutely ridiculous; I couldn't even go five hours without talking to my best friend, but he took the threat seriously and hadn't bugged me about it for the remainder of the summer.

Oliver was the guy that everyone liked. There was something about his personality that drew people in, a quality he got from his father. He was kind and fair to everyone. He had the looks, he had the heart, and honestly, I don't think there was a girl in school that could admit to not having a crush on him at one point in their lives.

"Can you please come and say thank you, Abbygail?" my mother scolded.

"Yeah, I'm coming."

"Are you okay?" Evelynn asked when I joined them under our carport.

I offered her the best smile I could muster. "I'm fine, just a little cold. Thanks for dinner, the ribs were great."

"You're so welcome, sweetheart." Henry took me in for a hug and over his shoulder, I spotted Oliver watching us.

"Goodnight, Uncle Henry."

He pulled away and threw me a knowing smile. "You're aware he's only teasing you, aren't you?"

"I am. And I have every intention of getting him back," I replied, confidently.

"I'm pretty sure you will. Goodnight, Abbygail, I'll see you tomorrow."

I watched Oliver hop on his skateboard, roll down my driveway and cross the street. "'Night, Monkey Butt. I hate you."

Hopefully he'd buy the teasing in my tone. I really didn't want him to know how much of what had happened under the willow tree affected me. He flipped me off as soon as he reached his lawn, but then turned around and grinned. "Hate you back, Freckle Face. Don't forget I'm picking you up tomorrow morning. You better be ready on time."

"I'm always on time," I rebuked.

He snickered. "No, Abby. You're not."

He was right, I wasn't, and I most likely wouldn't be when he'd be showing up at my door in the morning either.

When we were eight years old, Oliver and I came up with this idea: on the nights we couldn't sleep at each other's house, we'd show up at our bedroom window and wave goodnight. Eight years later, it had become a ritual, something we did without even thinking twice about it. But as I stood in front of my window that same night, I couldn't muster up the courage to turn my light on.

In the dark I watched him waiting for me. I thought about his mouth covering mine in a sweet tender kiss. How his lips tasted like the root beer slushy he'd bought us for desert. How I'd wanted more but wasn't able to tell him…

For the first time in my life I was disappointing my best friend. I wasn't doing it on purpose. I was prettified. Oliver had no idea what he had done when he put his lips to mine. What I felt for him was real, and I couldn't tell him. The risks were too high, and losing him was out of the question.

Love caused pain.

I saw it when my mother suffered through her heartbreak when my dad left us. She was broken, shattered, and I promised myself that I would never let something like that happen to me. I refused to have my heart broken like hers.

No matter what my heart desired, I wasn't going to lose my best friend. Nothing was worth jeopardizing our friendship. Not even love.

Especially not love.

CHAPTER TWO

OLIVER

"Okay, kid." My father stood in the bathroom door, leaning on the frame. "Tell me what's going on."

"Nothing," I mumbled. I had to go pick Abby up for school in less than twenty minutes, and instead of getting ready I stood fixated on my own reflection, wondering how I was going to face my best friend now that I had let my feelings for her win over my sense of reason

"Then why have you been staring at yourself with your toothbrush in your mouth for the past five minutes?" he asked, chuckling.

My father was the kind of man with whom you could sit down and talk about anything. He listened and never passed judgement on anyone. When I screwed up, he'd give me a chance to explain myself and if I fucked up, then he made sure the punishment was fair. Normally I had no issues talking with my dad. In this case however, no matter how close we were, this wasn't about some stupid thing I did or a bad grade, this was about Abby and everything I was feeling for her. And for some reason voicing it out loud would make it even more real than it already was.

When he saw that I wasn't going to open up, he arched a brow. "Oliver."

I spat in the sink and rinsed my toothbrush. "If I tell you about this, you have to promise me you won't make a big deal out of it. And you need to swear not to tell Mom. The last thing I need is for her to get mixed up in this."

He nodded, but I knew that the likelihood of him not telling her was slim to none. My parents were an open book with each other, especially when it came to me. Hopefully, he would be able to talk her down from her excitement. I had a feeling that the moment she found out I was in love for the first time in my life, she would be making a big deal out of it. The questions, the teasing, the relentless taunting...I'd never see the end of it. But the worse part was that she would tell Jenna, because those two told each other everything.

"I kissed Abby last night."

"I see." He didn't seem surprised at all. "And this makes you—"

"Nervous, anxious, stupid, happy?" I grabbed my hair with both hands and sat on the side of the bathtub. "I don't know. Enormously screwed."

"Come on, Oliver. Don't you think you're overreacting a little? I mean, we're talking about Abbygail Evens. You know her, she knows you… I really doubt this is a bad as you're imagining it to be." He walked over and sat by my side. "How did she react to the kiss?"

"That's the thing. I don't know."

"You don't know? How in the world can you not know? Did she kiss you back?"

"Um…Maybe? I'm not sure. It kind of happened really fast, and then I couldn't see her eyes, so I got nervous and left her under the willow tree."

"Did she say anything?"

"Besides calling me Monkey Butt? No. But she didn't show up in the window to wave goodnight last night like she normally does. I swear, Dad, I really think I screwed up this time."

He crossed his arms over his chest and beamed. Why he would smile while I was having a mental breakdown, was beyond me, but he was irritating the hell out of me.

"What makes you think you screwed up?" he asked, curiously.

I shrugged. "I don't know. I mean she's been acting really weird lately."

"Okay..." I could see it in his eye that he didn't want to push the matter, but I could also tell that he was curious. He waited for a response and when I didn't answer, he probed some more. "How was the kiss?"

I felt the thrumming inside my heart just thinking about it and smiled.

"That good, huh?"

I nodded.

"Then what's got you so worried?"

"She's my best friend."

"And?"

I frowned. "Best friends aren't supposed to kiss each other, Dad."

"Oliver, what would you say if I told you that Abby's at home right now probably having the same internal debate as you are?"

"I'd tell you that you're completely delusional."

He raised his brow, questioning me with his piercing gaze.

"What?"

"How much do you like Abby, son?"

Could I tell him that the girl I grew up with owned me heart and soul?

Would he scold me if I told him what I'd done to make sure no guy in school touched her?

I ran my hand through my messy hair, desperate

for the truth to finally be out. "I don't just like Abbygail, Dad. I want her to be mine. I love her."

There I said it.

Fuck this feels good.

"Then you have nothing to fear."

"How can you even say that? I have everything to fear. She's my best friend. What if she doesn't feel the same?" *What if I hurt her?* "I can't risk losing her."

"You won't. Abbygail loves you, Oliver. And I can guarantee that your friendship means more to her than you could possibly imagine. You two have a connection so rare that nothing could tear you apart. I swear, when you two are around each other it's like you're holding on to each other's next breath."

"Dad, Abby has this profound theory that all passionate relationships are doomed for failure."

"And what do you think?"

"Oh, I know she's wrong. But—"

"Then maybe you should try showing her."

"Really? And how would I manage that if she's convinced that she can't be in love without being hurt? What if I fail at being the person she needs?"

"She keeps you in her life because you're exactly who she needs you to be, Oliver."

"Fine then, what if in the process of wanting more, I hurt her and lose my best friend?"

"Do you have any intentions of hurting her?"

"Of course not, but let's get real, here, Dad, we're—"

"What if your fears are also hers, Oliver? Have you ever given any thought to that?" He raised his brow. "Give her some time to think. Let her feel and sort out what's going on in that beautiful mind of hers. I promise you that once she does, she'll come around. I would even be willing to bet you a thousand dollars that she feels the same way about you."

"A thousand, huh?

"Don't even think about it. You're going to lose the bet. And trust me if you do decide to go against me on this, I'll be using that thousand dollars in man-power. Now go get ready for school. I'm already late for work because of your daydreaming."

I laughed and he all but pushed me out of the bathroom.

"Thanks for the talk, Dad."

He threw me a proud smile. "Anytime, kid."

CHAPTER THREE

ABBYGAIL

I flipped my room upside down, desperately searching for my dark blue jeans, but they were nowhere to be found. Wearing nothing but a pair of underwear and my black belly button baseball jersey, I scanned the pile of clothing at my feet.

This is ridiculous... how can someone actually lose a pair of jeans?

"Mom?" I yelled, opening the door to my room. The sweet aroma of her famous banana muffins lingered in the hallway.

"Yes, sweetheart?"

"Have you seen my nice-ass-jeans?"

"First of all," she stretched her neck out from behind the wall of our kitchen. "Do not say *ass*. Second of all, how about you look in the pile of dirty clothes you left under your bed."

"I did. They aren't there. Was there a third of all?"

"Actually, yes, there is. When the hell did you start swearing so much?"

I crossed my arms over my chest and glared at her. "You're kidding me, right?"

"Abby, you add swear words between words."

"First of all, I do not. Second of all, did you even hear yourself talking right now?"

"I'm just trying to get my point across, Abbygail. Besides, I'm your mother, don't lecture me on the way I talk."

I rolled my eyes. "When's the last time you did my laundry?"

"When's the last time you brought it in the laundry room?"

I pursed my lips at her snarky comeback. "Uh…"

"Yeah, uh. Maybe you should always keep that room of yours that messy, Abbygail. Seems to me like it's the perfect way to find *everything* you're looking for." My mother and her sarcasm... She kept asking me where I got my attitude from but it was like she never listened to herself talk. "Abby, it's seven thirty, and you're still only half dressed. I have a patient coming in at eight thirty. I'm not driving you to school this morning."

"One day," I vowed, mumbling. "I'm going to record you."

"I heard that." she yelled.

I stepped back inside my room and shut the door behind me.

"Looks like someone's in a good mood."

I rolled my eyes unsurprised by the visitor sitting on my window frame. Oliver, who made a habit of climbing inside my house through my bedroom window whenever he felt like seeing me, was wearing his gray cargo shorts with a black fitted t-shirt. His dark hair was showing under the red Volcom baseball cap I'd bought him for his birthday.

As usual... hot.

He inhaled. "Mmmm. Did your mother make banana muffins?"

My brows pulled together as I nodded. It sort of dawned on me how still very much underdressed I was.

"What?"

"Any reason why you're sneaking up on me while I'm in my underwear?"

"Of course there is, but in my defense it's your own fault. You're late, and I thought you'd be ready."

"Clearly I'm not," I argued. "You could have used the front door instead of glaring at my ass while my back was turned."

"You wish I'd be glaring at your ass." I froze at his

teasing. "Besides, what's the difference between that and the bathing suit you wore last night?"

"It's a laced thong."

He shrugged as if he couldn't care less.

"You know," he said, hopping off the window framing. "Your mom's right: your room really is a fucking mess."

"Shut up, Ol, half the stuff in here belongs to you. Just—get out and let me get ready."

"With pleasure." He walked all the way to my door trying to avoid stepping on my things.

"Hey, Aunt Jen?" he yelled from my doorway. "Did you make an extra two for me?"

"You know I did," she chirped. "And I'll be more than delighted to give them to you as soon as you explain to me what your problem is with my front door."

"There's nothing's wrong with your front door, Aunt Jenna, I just really like your daughter's bedroom window."

"You do realize that she might decide to lock you out one day."

He chuckled, and glancing over his shoulder, he winked at me. "She wouldn't dare."

Annoyed by their conversation, I shook my head and when back to rummaging through the pile of clothing on my floor.

"Abbygail?" I let my focus shift his way. He was

watching me through the cracked door. "Your nice-ass-jeans are hanging in your closet."

"I thought you didn't care about my ass."

He grinned. "I don't. It's kind of big."

"I hate you."

"And I love you. Now get ready. We're going to miss the bus."

Giving myself a last glance in the mirror, I pulled my long dark hair up in a neat ponytail and added a black ribbon in a loose bow. Staring back at me was a girl with way too many little brown specks on her cheeks. I groaned, they were always worse at the end of the summer.

"Freckle Face, let's go," Oliver shouted from outside. "You have five more minutes to come out, or I'm leaving without you."

I walked up to my window and watched my best friend leaning on the huge rock in front of my house. He was basically stuffing his face with my mother's banana muffins.

"See if I care," I yelled back. "I'll just walk. Apparently, my ass needs the work."

He shook his head. There was something odd in his expression, I wish I knew what was going on in his head at that exact moment. He pulled his eyes away from his food and they landed on mine. The way he was looking at me made my heart flutter. I bit my bottom lip preventing my smile from cracking, but then he had to ruin the moment by raising his brow questioningly at me.

"Cut the self-conscious crap Abby. I'm your best friend. If I liked your ass, it'd be weird"

Whatever!

The split-level house my mother and I lived in was pretty big for two people, but it was the one I grew up in. I wouldn't have wanted it to be anywhere else. At one point, my father lived with us, but his presence didn't last very long. I was four years old when he bailed on our family.

My parents met during their last year of university. My mother was an aspiring dentist and Simon, my father, a journalist. Both had secured themselves good jobs even before their graduation. When Aunt Evelynn moved to B.C., my parents decided to move in together and bought a condo in Toronto. They lived happily ever after for a little over a year, and then I came into the picture ruining their perfectly content life.

A month before finding out that my mother was pregnant, Simon had applied for a job that would make him travel the world, something that apparently fascinated him, but that he never discussed with her until after he got the job. Unfortunately, my unexpected arrival was making a huge dent in his plans.

And then, I was born.

When my mother heard that the house across the street from her best friend was for sale, she managed to convince Simon that it would be a good idea to move away from the big city and settle into their first home as a family. Her best argument to convince him was that he was traveling so much for his work, and having Aunt Evy around could only be a positive aspect for our family. Conceding to my mother's desires, we moved into our home in Carrington. Unfortunately for my mom, her plan backfired.

My mother once told me that when I was born, Simon was okay with the idea of being a dad, but he travelled a lot, and as I grew up, he got better job opportunities. If he had to turn them down, he got angry. She did what she could to maintain balance in their relationship. She set her career aside for him and stayed home with me, but Simon was good at what he did, and he spent more time away than taking care of his family. I have a vague memory of them arguing over his constant lack of presence. Then one day, he just picked up and left. The day he left was the last time I saw him for years. He never wrote, he never called, no cards, no gifts... nothing.

My father's absence from my life had always been an issue for the both of us, but I guess in time I learned how to live with the fact that I ended up being last place on Simon's list of priorities. I often wondered what I did wrong, but most of the time, even though I never confronted her about it, I blamed my mother. I assumed that his decision to leave was related to an ultimatum she had imposed, because that's just the way she was: stubborn, just like me.

But in the end, I guess it didn't really matter. I had her, I had Aunt Evelynn and Uncle Henry, but most of all, I had Oliver. He kept me safe, he kept me sane and he was the one person I could count on, the one guy I trusted with my life.

"You're cleaning that room of yours as soon as you come back from school, Abbygail," my mother ordered. She was standing at the bottom steps waiting for me with my breakfast in her hand. "I'm sick and tired of always picking up after you."

I rolled my eyes. "Fine, I'll do it tonight, after Oliver's football practice."

I grabbed the muffin and kissed her on the cheek. "Have a nice tooth repairing day Mom!"

I shut the door behind me and faced my best friend who was grinning at me.

"Well, look who finally decided to step out fully dressed."

I groaned.

God this is going to be a long ass day...

CHAPTER FOUR

OLIVER

"What's with you?" I asked, annoyed.

We were walking up the street side by side in silence. She seemed angry. I was used to Abby's temper, but not so early in the morning, and normally it was a response to something I had done to piss her off.

And I hadn't done anything. Well, sort of.

"Nothing."

I grunted. "Sometimes I think you forget how much I know you. Here, give me your stuff, you'll be able to eat your breakfast."

"I don't need your help, Oliver," she snapped.

I pulled on her backpack making her take a step back.

"What the hell?" she complained. "We're going to miss the bus."

"Then we'll walk. Now, tell me what's wrong."

"You walked in on me half naked."

"So?"

She glared at me as if I was supposed to understand what her problem was, but the whole thing ended up infuriating me even more.

"How is today any different from any other day, Abby? I've seen you in your underwear all summer. I really don't see what the issue is. Plus, you were late, so if anything, it's your fault."

"You're kidding me, right? *You* climb up *my* bedroom window, and this ends up being my fault? Don't be so cocky, Oliver, you and I both know your reasoning doesn't even make any sense. You should have used the front door, then none of this would be happening."

"Are you shitting me? Are we really going to fight about me seeing you in your underwear right now?"

"Yes, Oliver, we are. And by the way, if you feel like I take too long to get ready in the morning: don't come over to pick me up. I'll remind you that I know where the bus stop is, and I don't need you to get there."

I let go of her bag and walked past her. "Whatever, Abbygail."

I am so done with this conversation.

"And you know what?" I say spinning on my heels.

"Next time you think about working on your beauty sleep, think about sparing some time for your *fucking bad temper.*"

She chucked her muffin at me and I caught it mid-air, earning myself a low growl.

I extended her breakfast with an open hand. "I play football, beautiful. Remember?"

She scowled and knocked my shoulder while she passed by me, not forgetting her muffin, which was a good thing otherwise I would have eaten it just to piss her off more.

Her silence told me that I may have overstepped my boundaries, but I wasn't going to back out on my comments. She had no reason to be this upset.

Smooth, Monkey Butt, real smooth.

I'll take that thousand bucks now, Dad.

ABBYGAIL

We reached the bus just as it pulled onto the corner. Oliver let me climb in before him as he usually did, but instead of taking the next available empty seat, I sat with Kylie.

My best friend stopped two seats away from me and raised his brow. "Are we really doing this?"

I crossed my arms over my chest and matched his annoyed stare. "We are."

"Suit yourself, Abbygail." He passed by me without giving me a side glance. Oliver knew he could have taken the empty bench beside ours, but instead he walked all the way to the back and sat with Zach.

As soon as the bus took off I regretted my decision of sitting with Kylie, and looked over my shoudler. For a fraction of a second his eyes met mine, and he creased his forehead, frowning angrily at me. I knew he had every right to be upset, but it didn't stop me from being irritated with him.

Or myself.

I wasn't even sure who I was really mad at anymore. The conflict I was having with myself didn't even make sense. I wished I could have told him that he was confusing the hell out of me with his teasing, and that his kissing me had only made matters worse. Everything would have been so much better if I could have told him everything I was feeling.

I returned my attention to the front of the bus.

I wish I could just tell you that I'm in love with you...

"Trouble in Love Paradise?" Kylie asked at the sound of my deep heavy sigh.

"Stop calling my relationship with Oliver, Love Paradise."

"Just calling it like it is, babe." Kylie was my closest friend. I bumped into her one morning when she was crying in the gym's bathroom. She had moved to Carrington in the middle of ninth grade and had a hard time getting used to our school, which totally made sense since everyone knew everyone here and outsiders were excluded more often than not.

She and I clicked instantly. I introduced her to Ava and Zoey, my childhood friends, and we quickly became the fantastic four.

What I appreciated the most about her was that she knew Oliver was my best friend. She understood that his presence in my life was a necessity, and she never showed any jealousy towards our relationship; unlike someone else in my circle of friends.

"So, tell me. Why aren't you sitting with your dreamy best friend?"

"Because he's an ass."

"Oh sure, that clears it up. What did he do this time?"

I looked over to the seat beside ours.

"Oh, come on," she scorned. "You can't blame this on him, Abbygail. You chose not to take the seat, not him."

"Ky, you don't even know what happened. And if you're going to take his side, then I don't want to talk about it." I picked at my banana muffin.

"How can you expect me to take sides if you don't tell me what the problem is?"

"Because I just told you. He's an ass." I completely

lost my appetite and chucked my food out of the window.

Kylie raised her eyebrow. Her hazel eyes were drilling holes through my skull, and as usual, her annoying gaze got me talking.

"Oliver kissed me last night."

"And you're pissed off at him because he kissed you?"

"No, Ky. I'm pissed off because of *why* he kissed me."

She didn't reply. She just looked at me as if I was the stupidest person on the earth.

I sighed. "He kissed me because he overheard our conversation about him yesterday after his football practice. Except he didn't know we were talking about him."

Thank God.

"He grilled me about what he heard all evening, and when he finally realized I wouldn't give in, he–"

"You should have just told him."

"Are you crazy? That's never going to happen. I already told you, Oliver and I are friends. That's it. And even if I do love him, I can't date him. If we screw up and I lose him, then I've got nothing left."

"Thank you," she answered sarcastically.

I shook my head. "That's not what I meant, and you know it."

"Abby, seriously, you're not making sense. It's what

you've been dreaming about for the past six months. And FYI, Oliver didn't kiss you to provoke you. He did it because he feels for you what you do for him."

"I know my best friend, Kylie. Trust me, you've got it wrong. Now can we please stop talking about this?"

"But you're wrong–"

"I said drop it, Ky."

"Fine." She opened her romance novel and left me to my thoughts.

I hated fighting with Oliver. A real argument between us rarely happened, but when it did, I felt like I couldn't breathe. I was always afraid he'd get fed up with me or decide that our friendship wasn't worth his time anymore.

"I know what you're thinking," Kylie said, lowering her book. "Stop worrying about it. You mean too much to him, Abs. You two will be back to your annoying selves before lunchtime."

Our town wasn't that big, but even then, the ten-minute drive to school felt as though it had lasted at least an hour. I tried to listen to the conversations in the back of the bus, but it was pointless. Once I realized that Oliver was as mute as I was, I stopped paying attention.

After dropping off the younger kids that went to the elementary school two blocks down from our school, the bus entered our student drop off. There were at least ten other buses leaving when we arrived. Many of the students that attended our school came from the surrounding townships, which explained why both schools and their grounds were as big as they were.

I grabbed my backpack and stepped out. Kylie and I joined Ava and Zoey by the bike racks. I assumed Oliver would be following close behind, since it was our usual meeting place.

"Good morning." Zoey cheered when she saw us approaching. She frowned when she noticed my demeanor, but didn't say a word.

Zoey was always bubbly about everything, the complete opposite of me. Her carefree spirit would always draw people in, and more often than not I found it annoying. She craved any attention or compliment she could get by implicating herself in anything and everything that was school-related. Her flaw, though, was like my own: we both had a very bad temper. I couldn't count the number of arguments she and I had gotten into. The main problem between us was that she had serious issues with my relationship with Oliver. I couldn't tell if it was because she didn't 'get' how close we were or if it was out of jealousy. I always suspected she liked him more than a friend, but I wouldn't be saying anything. Besides, if there was one thing I knew for sure, it was that Oliver didn't like

Zoey in that way at all. Picking a fight with her about it would have been plain stupid.

"Where are the guys?" Kylie asked.

"Tyler and Stephan are already inside," Ava answered. "They said they'd keep us seats in the auditorium. Hey, Oliver."

"'Morning, Ava."

Ava was the complete opposite of Zoey. Her kindness was effortless. Everyone loved her, and it wasn't because she tried. It was because that's who she was. Her open-mindedness had everyone constantly drawn to her. Her parents were rarely home because of their work, so it was her grandmother that took care of her. During the summer, she'd travel the world with them, which explained her free spirit.

She eyed me suspiciously. "Are you okay?"

I gave her a tight smile. "I'm fine. Can we go in now?"

CHAPTER FIVE

ABBYGAIL

The auditorium was packed when we stepped in. Our bus must have been the last one to arrive because there were barely any available spots left. If the guys hadn't come in when they did, we would never have been able to sit together.

Oliver grabbed my hand and pulled me aside. "Abby, can we talk?"

"Yo, guys. We're up here," Stephan called out.

"We'll talk later, okay?" I whispered to Oliver.

He held my hand, and I lifted my eyes to our friends sitting in the back row. It was typical for them to sit there. The farther away from the teachers they were, the happier they felt. We waved to let them know we'd seen them, but I also saw the huddle of cheerleaders sitting right beneath them and groaned. Adalynn was the first one I spotted, it was hard not to, she was already glaring at me and at my hand.

Swell, another year with Miss Bitchy Face.

I pulled back, and Oliver frowned. "I'm not going up."

"Why not?"

"Because I don't want to sit there. She's already shooting daggers at me."

He looked up and saw the cheerleading squad watching us. "You're exaggerating. She's not that bad you know."

"She's infatuated with you, Oliver. She hates me because we're always together. And honestly, I don't care what you think. Go sit with the guys, and if you still want to talk, we'll talk later."

"Oliver," Tyler yelled.

He wanted to go. The whole football team was up there and I could clearly see the debate he was having. I sighed and let go of his hand. "Just go."

OLIVER

I hesitated for a brief moment, but changed my mind when I side-glanced at my best friend. Abby was right: whatever I had to say and what we needed to talk about wouldn't be resolved during a school meeting. Whatever was going on between us needed to wait a couple of periods.

At least now she's talking to me...

"Where are the girls?" Stephan asked, bumping my fist.

"They sat somewhere else."

"Why?"

I shrugged. Neither of them needed to know what had happened in the last twenty-four hours. I was still trying to figure out if kissing Abby was a stupid idea or not.

Stephan and I were good friends way before elementary school. Our friendship started during the summer we were four years old when our parents made us play soccer. It was one season and we never played again after that. Our bond, on the other hand, remained strong. We did pretty much everything together. He was the running back for the school football team and our group clown. He always got a kick out of playing pranks, especially on the four girls that hung out with us.

Tyler, he moved to Carrington at the end of fourth grade so we weren't as close. He had a pierced lip and eyebrow, and most of the time, he kept to himself. Sometimes, I wondered if life at home was a bit difficult, but he wasn't much of a talker so we never really found out. We were good friends, but I always suspected he had a thing for Abby, and I didn't trust him.

"You look out of it this morning, dude," Tyler joked.

"Yeah, Abby and I got into it this morning."

"Again?" Stephan puffed a snort. "What's up with you two? It's like all you've been doing is arguing, lately."

"Trust me. I know. And I'm going to get to the bottom of it today–"

"Hey, Oliver."

"Hi, Adalynn. How was your summer?" Not that I cared. I was just making polite conversation as I usually did when it came to her or her friends. I didn't get what issues Abby had with her. Adalynn was always sweet.

"It was okay. How was yours?"

"Fun. I played football and skateboarded a lot, went swimming, hung out with Abby... you know the usual."

Speaking of Abby...

My eyes wandered from the blonde girl in front of me to the piercing blue eyes observing me. She was sitting two rows down at the far right of the room, and once I saw her, I got completely absorbed in her beautiful face. I smiled thinking about her perfect freckles, but she didn't return my smile.

"Oliver," Tyler was looking at me expectantly. "Adalynn just asked you something."

She did?

"Um, sorry. I didn't catch that."

Adalynn looked over to where I was looking and clicked her tongue. As soon as Abby saw us both watching her, she shook her head and shifted in her seat to face the front of the auditorium.

"I was just saying how much I've missed you, and how I would really like it if you'd take me out sometime. I'll give you my number if you want."

Yeah... I don't think so. And why is she petting my leg like I'm a freaking cat?

"Ladies and gentlemen."

Thank God. Saved by the school principal.

"I'm so happy to see you back and hope you've had a wonderful summer. As usual, we are committed to making this year better than the last. Of course, there will be a couple of changes, particularly in our teaching personnel and–"

I tuned out. There were many more interesting things to think about other than listen to Mr. Wilder talk.

TWO MONTHS AGO

"Oliver. Let go. Let go." Abby's giggling squeal could light up a damn room.

I grabbed her just after she hosed me down with icy cold water, and placing her over my shoulder, I carried her all the way to the pool with every intention of throwing her in.

"Please don't. I'm sorry." she laughed, barely able to catch her breath. *"I promise I won't do it again."*

"First of all, I don't believe you. Second of all, you should have thought about whatever is happening now before you decided to spray me with freezing water."

Her beautiful long, brown hair fanned over her shoulders, while her warm body crushed against mine. She extended her arms and begged me with her ocean blue eyes. *"Please?"*

"Forget about it, Freckle Face. You're doomed."

I grinned when she wrapped her legs around me, gripping my body as if she was holding on for dear life. I could feel her hot skin against mine, and the black bikini she was wearing was, to my delight, not leaving very much to the imagination.

My initial plan was to throw her in, but sensing my physical response to the closeness of our bodies, I held onto her and jumped into the pool.

Her legs were still wrapped around me when resurfaced from the bottom of the pool, and for a brief moment when her eyes met mine, it was like there were no other people in *the world but us. Biting her lower lip, she pulled a strand of hair out of my face and beamed. For a fraction of a second, I saw something in her eyes that I had never noticed, but before I could question anything she weaselled herself out of my grip and stepped out of the pool.*

Mid-way through the steps she turned around and gave me the most gorgeous smile I had ever seen. "I'm going to get you back, you know."

"I know." And I'm looking forward to it, too.

Stephan called my name, pulling me out of my daydreaming.

"What?" I grumbled, annoyed.

"You're staring at her again."

"Who?"

"Seriously?" He chuckled. "Abbygail, dumbass."

"No I wasn't."

Was I? Yeah, I probably was...

"Did she notice?"

"Nah man. You're cool. She was completely engrossed in our new gym teacher, Mr. Camdon. Where were you anyway?"

"First of July, Abbygail, small black bikini, pool–"

"Ah. Say no more. I remember that day very well."

I punched his shoulder. "Dude, do not think of Abby like that."

"You're the one that brought it up," he fired back, grinning.

"Maybe, but I wasn't having dirty–"

He raised his brow calling me out on my lie before it even came out.

"You know what? Never mind. Is this thing over yet?"

He nodded.

Thank god.

CHAPTER SIX

OLIVER

"So, where to now?" I asked Stephan walking down the lecture hall's busy stairs.

He, Tyler, and I wormed our way through the crowd and stopped at the first table. "Code of conduct, timetable, student ID picture, lockers, recess, class, lunch... Do I need to go on?"

"No. I got it thanks"

"Hey Oliver wait up." I heard calling behind me.

I turned to see Adalynn waving at me and sighed. Adalynn was nice, but she lived in a fantasy world where she thought football players should be dating cheerleaders exclusively. She had gone through a lot of team members already, and I had no intention of being her next victim. Although pretty: long blonde hair, piercing green eyes... she just wasn't my type. And no matter how many times I tried to turn her down, she always came back. She was persistent, I had to give her that.

"So, have you thought about it?" Adalynn demanded, rubbing her shoulder against mine.

"Thought about what?"

"The date."

I saw Stephan's smirk when I rolled my eyes. "Um–"

"And you are?" My ninth-grade math teacher asked.

He's joking right?

"Oliver Langton, advanced mathematics, always sat in the back row. How can you not remember an awesome face like mine, Mr. Fontaine?"

He chuckled. "Of course, Oliver. I'm sorry I wasn't really looking."

I watched him study me. He didn't have a damn clue who I was. The older he got, the more I was beginning to think he was losing his memory.

"Here's your schedule, important papers to read, and forms for your parents to fill out. Go take your I.D. picture over there and you're all set. Oh, and if you need help with your math class this year, drop by the math office, Oliver, I'll be more than happy to help. Have a great school year."

I glanced at my timetable and shook my head; I'd be seeing him first period after lunch.

"Hey Oliver, wait up," Adalynn called out as I stepped away from the teacher who assigned me my locker.

I groaned.

"Here, I almost forgot." She grabbed my right hand and wrote her phone number in my palm. I could have just taken it away, but for some reason, I just stood there letting her do whatever she needed to do. Besides, I knew very well my next stop would be the restrooms to wash it off.

"Don't forget to call," she whispered, leaning in on me.

Before backing away, she left a soft lingering kiss on my cheek. I was stunned. Completely unable to move. She stepped away with a wide smile on her face and left without saying a word. As for me, well, I blinked twice and the second I reopened my eyes, I noticed Abby standing a few students behind me, watching what I had let happen.

ABBYGAIL

All I wanted to do was to smash Adalynn's face against the wall when she passed with a proud grin.

I didn't.

I did what I did best when it came to her: I looked at the floor. And funnily enough, I did the same when I walked passed Oliver. I couldn't even tell if he tried to reach out to me or not. I lost all focus or any ability to breathe until I was far enough to regain my composure.

"She kissed him," I whisper-yelled when Kylie joined me.

"I know. I saw. Are you okay?"

"No, Kylie. I'm not okay. What was he thinking?"

"He? He didn't do anything, Abs. Adalynn kissed him. And in his defense, I'm pretty sure he didn't reciprocate."

"*Who cares*? She kissed him." I kicked the nearest locker. "And why have you been sticking up for him so much lately?"

"Because I don't feel like you have a legitimate reason to be mad at him."

"Why not?"

"Because he didn't do anything wrong, Abby."

"You should think about becoming a defense attorney," I scowled.

"Maybe I will," she laughed. "Let's go now. We need to find our lockers."

"Do you think the person in my locker will want to

switch with us?" I asked Kylie as we unloaded our bag. We got lucky, we were only five doors apart from each other.

"You don't even know whom you're paired up with yet."

"I don't think I'll care who it will be. Besides, there aren't too many people that tolerate my messiness."

"*I* don't tolerate your messiness." she replied, shutting her door.

"OMG! Did you just see Adalynn kiss Oliver?" Zoey exclaimed the second she saw us. "The whole school will be talking about this by lunch time."

I cursed under my breath.

"Zoey, don't," Kylie reprimanded.

All three pairs of eyes were on me, but only one dared to continue. "Oh come on, Abby. You're not his girlfriend, you're his best friend. You do realize he's one of the hottest guys in school, and he's single? It's like you don't want him to have any fun."

"I hate her, Zoey. You know that already."

"Then it's a good thing you're not the one that's going to date her."

I frowned.

"He's not going to date her. He doesn't even like her," Ky bit back.

"Really, Kylie? How could you possibly know that?"

"I just do, Zoey. Now quit it."

I crouched down and tried to stop their

conversation from getting to me. The only one who hadn't said anything was Ava. She just looked at me with a worried expression on her face. She and Kylie were the only ones who knew how I truly felt about my best friend.

"Abs?" Ava whispered.

I looked up to her and she nudged her head forward. Oliver was walking up our row. I stood up so fast, my knees cracked. Facing him was the last thing I wanted, but the first thing I should have expected. "Guys. Could you just please shut up?"

Both stopped bickering and ogled me like I'd grown a pair of horns. I had no idea what they were arguing about anymore, but honestly, I didn't care. The last thing I wanted was for Oliver to know what was going on between us.

"What's your deal, Abbygail?" Zoey snapped.

"My deal, Zoey, is that you should know how much I hate that girl, and you should also know how much she despises me. She's going to make my life a living hell. But if you're going to support Bimbo Blondie, then just go over there and be a pompom girl. We are *all* done talking about this."

She glared at me and spun around, coming face-to-face with my best friend.

"Done talking about what?" Oliver inquired.

"Nothing." Three of us declared at the same time.

Zoey just stared at him and batted her eyelids like she always did.

"Okay..." He paused and squinted at me. I knew I'd be going through a whole lot of questioning as soon as the girls would be dismissed. "I'm going to need you to step aside."

"Why?" I frowned

"Because if you don't, I won't be able to put my things away in our locker."

"Our locker?" I asked surprised. "How did you manage that?"

"It's the Langton's charm. Hey girls, would you mind if I stole my bestest friend ever for the next ten minutes or so?"

"Please do." Zoey answered. "I'm out. We'll talk later."

I studied Oliver while he unpacked. I couldn't believe he was able to charm a teacher into switching lockers.

"Do you still want to switch partners?" Kylie whispered just loudly enough for me to hear.

I shook my head and smiled at her.

"I thought so." Her lips curled upwards. "We'll talk later. Come on, Ava. Let's go see what's up Zoey's panties this morning."

I leaned on the metal door behind me and watched both of them walk away. When they rounded the corner, I raised my eyes to meet Oliver's. He was leaning on his arm above my head, staring at me intently. He was so close, his face literally inches from mine, and it took me everything to breath steadily.

"We need to talk." His tone was stern, and I swallowed nervously. "Do I want to know what that was about?"

"Um… No you don't." My voice quivered. "Girl drama?"

He eyed me suspiciously, trying to read me. I could tell because of the way he peered down at my eyes.

I didn't even know what I was feeling anymore; my heart was juggling anger, jealousy, happiness and fear. "I see you finally got rid of your fawning harem." I pulled away. Being so close to him was driving me crazy.

He took his last binders out of his back pack and dropped them on the top shelf. "A harem is composed by more than one person, Abby."

"Who cares about definitions, Oliver?" I sneered. "I saw you. Do not stand there and deny that satisfied look on your face when Adalynn was hanging on your arm or when her hands were all over your body in the auditorium."

"Satisfied look? I was annoyed, Abbygail. Of all people, you should know the difference."

"You kissed her."

"She kissed me."

"Same fucking thing."

"No, Abby. It's not."

"Are you going to call her?"

"Eww, God no. And I'm actually insulted you think so little of me. Clearly, you have no idea what kind of girl I like."

"Please. You're a sixteen-year-old guy. You like anything with boobs and long legs."

"That was totally uncalled for. What's it to you, anyway? Jealous much?"

"Jealous? Me? Uh, no."

God yes.

"If you think I'm jealous of a blonde bimbo cheerleader that smooches your face and pets your leg to get your attention, you are totally mistaken."

"Well, if you ask me, the fact that you noticed *any* of her doings proves the opposite, *Abbygail*."

"It proves nothing. I hate her. The fact that she's trying to weasel herself into your pants and that you're letting her infuriates me. And stop calling me Abbygail with that tone. It annoys me."

"First of all, I can call you whatever I want and however I want. It's the privilege of being your best friend."

I snorted.

"Second of all, I'm not *letting* her do anything. I don't like her like that, Abby. For fuck's sakes. Could you just tell me what's going on with you this morning, so we can move on from it?"

"Nothing."

"Cut the shit, Abs," he replied, slamming the door. "You've been pissed off at me since this morning, and I have no fucking clue what I did wrong. If you're going to be mad at me, don't you think I should at least know why?" His index finger and thumb held my chin up to his face. "Tell. Me. What's. Wrong."

He was close. So close. I could feel my heart wanting to beat itself out of my chest. I looked at his eyes, at his lips and then back at his eyes again.

If I tell him, it will be a disaster...

I bit my bottom lip trying to shake my head.

"Don't do that."

"What?"

"That. The bottom lip thing."

I frowned and then laughed. "Why?"

"I don't know. It–"

"Abby?"

Both of our heads veered to the other end of the row of lockers. "Is that my mom?"

Oliver chortled. "I think so."

I groaned.

This has got to be the most humiliating thing I have ever experienced in my entire life.

"Abbygail?"

Why is my mother screaming my name? What could I have possibly done to deserve this? This is the first day of school... and I'm in the middle of a super important conversation.

"Abbygail, there you are," my mother puffed. "We need to–"

Did I forget something this morning? My keys? My lunch? No. I just put my lunch into my locker before Oliver got here. Didn't she have a patient at the clinic this morning?"

"ABBYGAIL." My focus shifted back to my mother. "Have you not heard anything I just said? I'm bringing Oliver to the hospital."

Huh?

"Why?"

"I really wish you'd listen to me when I talk once in a while."

And I wish you didn't show up at school shouting my name like a mad-woman, but we can't all have what we want now, can we?

"Henry's been in a car accident, Abby."

My worried eyes crossed my best friend's. "Is he okay?"

"I don't know. Are you coming with us or not?"

I grabbed his hand and frowned at my mother.

Talk about a stupid question!

CHAPTER SEVEN

ABBYGAIL

The drive to the hospital was silent. I chose to sit on the back seat with Oliver instead of the front seat with my mom because who was I kidding, there was nowhere else I would rather be.

Oliver was good at keeping his self-control. The only sign of stress he showed was his left leg bouncing while lost in his own thoughts, he stared at the ongoing traffic outside. I wanted to say something, but nothing seemed appropriate.

Deep down, all I wanted was to tell him everything was going to be okay, but it felt wrong the last thing my best friend needed was for me to lie to him. I stretched out my hand and interlaced my fingers with his. As soon as our touch met, he lost his focus and turned his sad eyes to mine, then to our joined hands.

"Oliver?" I whispered. I didn't say anything more; I simply lifted our combined hands to my lips. With a silent nod he pulled me closer to him and placed them back on his thigh.

The unsteadiness of his heartbeat was the only thing I heard while we silently held on to each other.

OLIVER

The drive to the hospital took fifteen minutes. I knew this because I checked the time when Aunt Jenna put the keys into the ignition of her Mercedes. The Evens' must have been as anxious as I was because no one had said a word since Abby and I left our locker.

The silence was eerie. The only sound we heard was the voice of Amy Lee playing on the radio as she sang her part of *Broken* by Seether.

Abby and I holding each other was the only thing that kept me grounded. For a brief moment, when we were at school and she wasn't paying attention to her mother, I actually believed that she had been so angry with me that she wouldn't come to the hospital with us. But having her heart beating so closely to mine made me realize how, even the thought of it, was ludicrous. Our morning argument had completely dissipated into thin air, giving room for more important things.

It was then that I understood that my father was right: nothing could tear us apart. This girl had no idea how much I needed her.

I straightened my spine when I saw that we had arrived at the hospital. "Aunt Jen, can you drop me off at the emergency entrance?"

Sensing my nervousness Abbygail pulled away from my shoulder, but didn't let go of my hand.

Jenna hesitated. I knew she would have preferred our going in all together, but I wasn't patient enough to wait. I begged her silently, and conceding to my desires, she dropped Abby and me at the door and took off with a faint tire screech. Facing the revolving doors, my best friend released a loud sigh, linked her fingers with mine again, and together we walked in.

The entrance to the hospital was a drab gray and brownish color. It was poorly lit, uninviting and stank of cleaning products and sick people. The place was loaded with patients waiting in line. I groaned. The last thing I wanted to do was to wait for my turn. It seemed like such a waste of time.

As if she read my thoughts, Abby exhaled loudly. "This is ridiculous. I'm not waiting in line. Stay here."

She walked off a few meters away and addressed the awkward security guard standing a few feet away. I watched her talk animatedly and chuckled when she signaled me to join her. I had to hand it to Abby: more often than not she knew how to use her temper to our advantage.

"Come on." She grabbed my arm. "We need to go to the trauma unit. It's on the second floor."

I wanted to take the elevator. Something about her words scared me, and I didn't think my legs could carry me up there. Unfortunately for me though, Abby dragged me along with her, claiming we had wasted enough time. Together, we climbed the stairs, two by two, until we reached the door to the second floor.

As much as downstairs was dark, the second floor, was the complete opposite. The walls were cream colored with bright fluorescent lights, and the smell... it was as bad as the ground floor but worse in some way. The antiseptic seemed stronger, more present. I hated it.

Walking together side-by-side, we turned left, and the deserted corridors became chaos. The scene made me dizzy as I stood motionless, searching for my mother. Employees were running around, worried family members sat holding each other while others paced impatiently, kids cried...

Without hesitation Abby, let go of my hand and walked up to the nursing station. It was a good thing I had her, otherwise, I would have been completely lost. "Hi."

The nurse looked up from her desk.

"My friend's dad was just in a car accident, and we're looking for his mother."

"What's the patient's name?"

"Henry Langton."

I noticed grief in the nurse's face when Abby named my dad. I frowned at her, trying to figure out what was behind her sad demeanor, but she was quick to recover and looked on her computer.

Get a grip Oliver...

"You may go to room two seven five, but Miss, you can't go with him. Only immediate family members are allowed in the area."

Abby rolled her eyes at the nurse. "Fine… I'll just follow him and not go in."

"I'm sorry, Miss, you can't–"

I gave the nurse a mean glare and grabbed Abby's hand.

If that woman thinks I'm walking there alone without Abby, she's fucking delusional. I don't care who you are, you are not keeping my best friend away from me right now!

We could hear the nurse hollering at us when she saw that I chose to ignore her request, but neither one of us slowed down until we were far enough away to not to hear her anymore.

As we turned the corner, we both came to realize that the room the nurse had instructed us to go to was in a very secluded and quiet hallway.

"Oliver." Abby tried to let go of my hand, but I gripped tighter. I was on edge and wouldn't have been able to let go even if I wanted to.

I didn't want to.

"I'm going to wait here for you," she whispered. Her voice was unsteady. It was like she knew something that I didn't.

"Please don't let go," I pleaded.

She nodded sadly, and I knocked on the slightly ajar door. It opened gently and I saw my mother sitting alone on one of two plastic blue chairs. What I was seeing was nothing I expected. I couldn't understand why my mother was sitting in that room all alone and not by my father's side.

Hunched over herself, she was leaning on her elbows holding her head. I'd never seen my mom so broken. She had always been full of light, and joy. Now, her eyes and face were puffy and red, and she was shaking.

"Mom?" I questioned.

She looked up. It took a while before she realized that I was the one she was looking at, but as soon as the realization hit her, she let out a loud sob and threw herself into my arms. Part of me understood what was going on, but the other part wanted to remain in denial.

"Mom, where's Dad?"

Hearing nothing but her muffled cries, tears began

to pour out of my eyes. She held onto me even tighter, but she was shaking so much it felt like I was holding onto her rather than the other way around.

I pushed her away slightly, needing to see her face. All she had done since I opened the door was avoid my gaze. "Mom, where is he?" My voice was filled with rage.

She refused to answer, or maybe it was because she was unable to. I had no idea.

"Mom." I yelled louder.

She backed away from me.

"You can't keep him away from me. I want to see him."

She shook her head as she cried. Her inability to explain what was going on enraged me, so I shook her shoulders frantically. Finally getting her attention, she looked up at me. She seemed frightened, but I didn't care.

"I want to see him. WHERE IS HE?"

"I'm so sorry Ol–Oliver."

She was barely able to articulate her thoughts. I frowned. She was sobbing so much I couldn't understand what she was saying. I heard something that sounded like *'he was running late...in a hurry...got ran into by a truck...'* but I knew I must have misheard her.

She wiped her nose with her shirt and stopped when she realized what she was doing. There were so many questions hidden behind her eyes. And then, as if the whole situation had just hit her, she gave a serious stare. "He's gone."

There are so many things in life a teen doesn't want to live through. Losing a parent definitely made the top three of my list. Having to hear from my mother's lips that I had the last conversation I would ever have with my dad that morning broke my heart in two.

As the tears of pain and agony ripped through my broken soul, I held on to the only person I thought would prevent my life from shattering into a million pieces. She held me in her arms, mixing her tears with my own.

I begged her to tell me it was all just a dream. She didn't.

I begged her to wake me up, and when she said she couldn't to do it, I begged her to tell me it was all just a lie. She didn't.

I begged her to ignore everyone around us and to help me find my father. She hugged me even tighter, rocking our bodies, holding me, preventing me from crumbling to the floor as best she could.

It wasn't working.

The pain and the tears… the ache was too much to handle.

"Abby. It hurts. Please just make it stop."

She pulled her hands up to my cheeks and held my

face, leaning her forehead on my own. Her breath was warm and shaky. Her eyes were so clear I couldn't bear looking at them, so I closed mine.

I wanted to drown in the darkness. "Abs. Please."

She leaned in and kissed my temple. "I–I can't, Oliver."

"But it's not true, Abs." I reopened my eyes. "I'm telling you, they're lying to us. He's here somewhere. I know he is. I–come with me please," I beseeched standing up and extending my hand for her to take. "I need to see him. I need to talk to him."

She looked so broken sitting on the floor.

Staring at her crystal blue eyes, willing her to believe me, willing her to understand that I needed her to believe me, she finally took my hand, and for that fraction of a second, I felt hope.

"Oliver." She glanced at my mother who simply shook her head sadly. "I–" Her eyes ascended from our joined hands to my eyes, locking her throbbing heartache to mine. "Oliver, I can't… he's gone."

I felt like I was in a trance. If my own best friend wouldn't believe me, then I had nothing.

"Oliver?" she asked once I pulled my hand away from hers.

I looked at her sitting on the ground and felt nothing. I felt empty. I turned and walked away.

"Oliver," she repeated.

She must have gotten up pretty fast because she

was standing in front of me even before I made it to the corner of the waiting room.

"Look at me," she implored.

I ignored her.

"Oliver," she pleaded with a wavering voice. "Please…"

"I'm done, Abby," I replied without looking back.

"You're done? Done with what?"

"Them, him, you, us…I'm done." I turned around and met her beautiful broken eyes. "I'm done with all of it."

ABBYGAIL

As I stood alone in the middle of the quiet hallway, I watched my fragmented best friend walk away from me.

"Time." my mother whispered. "It's what he needs, Abby,"

With everything that had just happened, I hadn't even noticed she made it upstairs.

"Just let him go. You'll talk once we get home," she reassured me, taking me in for a much needed hug.

From the corner of my eye, I watched Oliver walking away from us. I yearned for him to stay, but he never looked back.

The difficult part of seeing my best friend in pain was to watch his heart break and not being able to do anything about it.

The hardest part was to realize just how much he hated me for it.

CHAPTER EIGHT

ABBYGAIL

Henry was more of a dad to me than my own father ever was. He took care of my mother and I. He welcomed us into his life like we were his own family.

He was the one who taught me how to ride a bike, showed me how to ice skate, took me camping and fishing... he was the one who listened to me when I needed to talk about anything. And now... he was gone.

The devastation of his death felt ten times worse because I didn't have my best friend to grieve with. From the moment Oliver turned that corner at the hospital, he made himself scarce. He didn't call, he didn't come over, and he never showed up to say goodnight at the window. He did nothing but hide from me, and every time I knocked on his door, Aunt Evelynn said that he didn't want to see me.

It stung. All I wanted was to sit and cry with him. I understood that the loss of his father was hard, but I didn't understand why he was avoiding me, especially since he and I were suffering the same loss.

I could hear my mother and Evelynn's quiet sobs as they sat side by side in church. I envied their closeness. My mother supported her best friend in her sorrows while *my* best friend had purposefully chosen the seat by the aisle. There were only two people between us, but the distance that separated us felt like he was all the way across the country.

I attempted to listen to the pastor, but between dealing with my own grief and trying to look out for my best friend, I couldn't focus. I was never a religious person. I believed in what I saw and how it made me feel. I believed in life. The closest I came to praying was when my mother made me do it on special occasions, and even then, I sucked at it. So, as I sat there on the uncomfortable wooden pew, all I could really think about was how angry I was at life and how it was unfair that Oliver's dad was taken away from us.

I tried to understand the man and his words of

wisdom, but to me, everything he said sounded like load of bullshit.

When the ceremony drew to an end, I was asked to come forward and talk about the man we had all lost. The day before the funeral, Aunt Evelynn had asked me to speak about Uncle Henry. She said she knew it would have made him happy to know how much he meant to me, but also to us as a family. In truth, it was an honor, but I didn't know if I could truly do his life justice.

Standing in front of the church, I noticed how much Oliver's dad had been loved. Aside from my teary friends who sat together a few seats behind ours, the church held many family members, co-workers, people from our community, and many other people I didn't recognize.

I looked down at my sheet of paper. What I had written the previous night was everything I had ever wanted to tell the man I'd considered as my dad, but had never had the chance to. I wrote how fantastic I thought he was and how much he was going to be missed, detailing the happy memories and telling everyone how his being in my life was a gift. I wrote how anyone who had ever been lucky enough to cross his path should feel blessed. And then, right before I opened my mouth, I dared to look at my best friend and everything got blurry.

"I don't have a dad," I started with a sad smile.

"Everyone has a dad. That's what you said. *It's how we make babies."*

A low rumbled laughter filled the room. I was happy I could make them laugh at such a difficult time, but my attention was focused on Oliver. I didn't care about the others. This was for him.

His face remained fixated on the church floor. I couldn't tell if he was paying attention to what I was saying or if he was just lost in his own thoughts.

"That's not what I meant." I continued, recalling the conversation we had so many years ago. "I mean that my own father never comes to see me. It's like he doesn't want to be my dad anymore. And then you said: *Well if you ask me, your dad's a jerk. I'm going to ask my dad if he can be your dad too."* A tear slipped my eye. "So, I have to ask. Did you?"

I didn't address him by name, but I knew he understood the moment he stood.

"Because I think you did," I rushed. "And I need to thank you."

I should have just stuck with what I wrote yesterday...

I looked over at my mother and her friend. "I'm sorry..." I blubbered. "I–I don't think I can do this."

Both looked at me with an understanding sad smile.

Oliver was no longer beside them. He had made it all the way to the back of the church, putting even more distance between us. Words got caught in my throat. I really needed Oliver to know what I had to say. "Uncle Henry–"

My best friend's eyes met mine just as he put his hand on the handle of the massive wooden doors. It was the first time he looked at me in days. Excluding the redness, I saw no emotion. His jaw was set, his face expressionless.

"Uncle Henry, I–" I didn't even know what to say next. I stared at my shaking hands and ended up blurting out the first thing that came to mind. "I need my best friend."

The church doors closed behind him and uncontrollable tears pooled out of my eyes.

He left...

I might have been devastated by the loss of the only dad I ever knew, but somewhere deep down, I also had the horrible feeling that I was grieving the loss of my best friend.

After the service was over, the pastor invited anyone who wanted to say their last goodbyes to join him in the cemetery behind the church. Since Oliver had left before the ending of the ceremony, I took on the responsibility of bringing our mothers. When I got there, I spotted Oliver at least fifty feet away from his father's grave, standing with his back to the church. His head faced the drizzling sky as if he was trying to rid himself of the pain. I let go of our mothers' arms and walked over to him.

He didn't look at me, but for the first time in days, he didn't shy away from my presence. "You're going to get wet, Abby."

"How do you know I don't have an umbrella?"

"You never carry an umbrella."

"If you know I never carry an umbrella, then you should also know I like the rain."

"You hate rain," he stated.

True... But I'll take standing in the rain with you over being dry without you anytime.

I sighed. "How did you know it was me?"

"Because I felt you. I can always feel you," he replied as if the answer was the most obvious thing on the planet.

"Is that a bad thing?"

Something in the way he stood away from me made me nervous, and I felt the tears welling up in my eyes all over again.

"Oliver, could you–could you look at me?" I needed to see his face. I needed to see that we were okay.

He turned his gaze to mine. His darkened orbs were blotchy and his face was wet. Itching to touch him, I reached out and shakily pushed a strand of hair away from his eyes. He unexpectedly leaned into my touch, pulled his hands out of his pocket, and wiped away the tears from my cheeks.

"I *need* to feel you, Abby," he finally replied.

I exhaled, relieved.

"Here," I said extending the orchid I was holding in my other hand.

He took the flower and rolled the stem between his index and his thumb.

"Beautiful," he said as he examined it closely. "Just like you."

My next breath caught in my throat. Trust Oliver to find a way to make me feel better on the day I was supposed to be supporting him.

"It's for your dad," I replied, confused. "Will you come with me?"

"I can't—"

"Of course you can. We'll do it together. I'll hold your hand while we say our goodbyes."

I sensed his hesitation. Saying goodbye to his dad was also the last thing I wanted to do.

But we needed to.

It's what people do when a loved one dies.

"I miss him," he said, huge tears spilling over his sunken cheekbones.

"I know. I do, too."

"Promise you won't let go?"

I extended my hand, and he took it. "I promise I will *never* let go."

Oliver held my hand tightly as we made our way back to our family and friends, but I didn't mind. The fact that he was letting me be there for him was more than enough. We walked up to his father's grave, and Stephan, Tyler, Kylie, Ava and Zoey joined us. As he and I knelt down, our friends stood closely behind us. Together, we watched as Oliver laid the orchid on his father's urn and said his silent farewells.

My heart broke as my best friend's body shook. If I had been able to, I would have taken away his pain and carried it with me forever.

"You gave a hell of a nice speech," Oliver tease when we made our way away from the crowd.

"You should have stayed until it was over," I replied, smiling just a little bit. "The end was epic."

"I did."

Oliver and I had made it far enough from everyone to be out of ear shot. He pulled to a complete stop, and I studied him, wondering if he had really heard my whispering pleads.

"The one on the paper was better," I admitted.

"I doubt it." He pulled his arms around my small body and hugged me. "Thank you for doing this with me."

"You're my best friend, Oliver. I'd do anything for you."

"I know," he said as he turned towards the burial site. Our friends had left. Only close family members stood by the graveside. "I'm going to head home."

"Can I walk with you?" It was more of a request than a question, but he shook his head and let go of my hand.

"I hope you know how much I love you, Abby," he whispered, leaving a soft kiss on my temple. "I'll see you at the house."

After he crossed the street, I looked up to the dark, gray sky and let the heavy rain fall over me. Alone, I cried and prayed for the aching pain to be washed away with the stream, but it didn't help. I don't know how long I stood there, but it was long enough for the wind to pick up and for my mother to call me to get inside over ten times.

I could feel the storm coming as I walked back to my mother's car. The rumbling thunder stopped me and I looked up again at the clouded sky. "Uncle Henry, please don't stop watching over us."

CHAPTER NINE

ABBYGAIL

We had all been invited to Zoey's house since her parents were gone for the weekend. I was pretty sure Oliver didn't want to come, but I texted him anyway in the hope of convincing him otherwise. Sure enough, he refused to join us, but about an hour into the party I saw him sitting on a bar stool in the kitchen with a Corona in his hand and Adalynn rubbing up against him.

He seemed happy, fitting perfectly with his football teammates.

Jealousy bubbled inside of me. I didn't get it. I didn't get him. As much as I tried to want to understand, it was no use. We were his friends. Why he chose to surround himself with other people that weren't us, I couldn't comprehend.

I'm his best friend...

He let her rub the back of his hair with her fake nails, and her proud smile spoke a thousand words she wouldn't dare say in his company.

My heart snapped.

When I made my way to the kitchen, Adalynn was the first one to see me. As soon as she saw my face, she smiled evilly and leaned over to whisper in Oliver's ear. He shook his head and smiled at her. It took a lot of self-control to ignore what was going on inside of me, but somehow, I managed to bury it down low enough, and pretend that everything was okay.

"Hello there Abbygail," Adalynn said as soon as I opened the door to the fridge.

Oliver's head shot up from the bottom of his beer bottle as soon as he heard my name leave her lips and he shrugged Adalynn's hand off his shoulder. Although his reaction made me smile a little, I never replied to her questionable greeting. Instead, my eyes were glued onto my best friend's dark stare.

"I thought you didn't want to come," I reached inside the fridge for anything to drink. I wasn't even thirsty. It was just better for me to have something in my hands, rather than regret doing something with my fists.

"Oh we weren't going to," Adalynn interrupted

Oliver before he could even respond. "But I managed to convince him after we went for dinner at the Diner."

I frowned, which was exactly the reaction she was looking for. She was just waiting for my response, but I once again swallowed my words—and the pain my best friend was inflicting to my heart—with the fruity drink I had in my hand.

"A couple of the guys from the team thought it would be cool if I joined them and the cheerleaders for dinner after practice," Oliver offered as an explanation.

Taking in his lousy excuse, I nodded silently. Oliver didn't go to practice.

He noticed the hurt on my face and for a fraction of a second, I saw the regret on his, but instead of responding, I offered him a tight smile and left the kitchen without saying a word.

"So that's where you're hiding." I heard calling from the side of the house. Stephan and Kylie were walking past the corner of the garage.

Since I couldn't take the pain of watching Oliver and the Pompom Bitch together anymore, I walked out of the front door and sat alone on the stone ramp of Zoey's front porch.

I gave them a pathetic smile. "Hiding would require

me not being in plain sight, Stephan. Where were you two anyway?"

"Out looking for you," he answered. "We didn't see you step out. What's with the gloomy face?"

"I just witnessed Adalynn getting nice and cozy with Oliver."

Stephan shook his head and took a seat on the ramp beside me. "Come on, Abs, you know just as much as I do that if he's letting her get close it's because he's drunk. You're the only person he ever lets in."

I wanted to believe him, but the fact was, Oliver and I had been so estranged that I didn't know what to believe anymore. Two weeks had gone by since Henry's passing, and Oliver was still refusing to see me. Our moment at the cemetery was the last time we had truly talked. When he'd gone back to school a week after the funeral, he did pretty much anything he could to make himself scarce. He skateboarded to and from school. He never bothered to pick me up, so we had absolutely no chance of spending any time together. Our encounter at our locker was basically the only time he chose to acknowledge me. The fact that he hadn't asked to switch lockers was my only comfort in knowing that whatever was going on would be temporary.

Something was up with him and it bugged the hell out of me that he wouldn't tell me what was going on.

"Abby," Kylie added. "You're reading way too much into this. Just go talk to him."

"And say what? I'm so pissed off at him right now, Ky. He said he didn't want to come yet here he is—"

"He probably just changed his mind, Abs," Stephan interrupted. "At least give him a chance to explain himself. I swear you two really drive me nuts sometimes. You do get that the concept of being best friends suggests that you need to talk to each other once in a while, right?"

"You don't think I've tried that already?"

"He needs you, Abby. You just need to remind him that you're still there and show him that you have no intention of giving up on him."

I sighed and rubbed the deep creases on my forehead away. "Fine." I pulled my legs around and stepped back on the porch. "I'll go check on him. Again. Oh, and hey," I called before walking inside the house. "Have any of you seen Tyler tonight?"

"He couldn't come," Stephan answered. "Something about his dad leaving town, I think. He was pretty vague about the whole thing. You know how he is about his family."

I did, and I also knew that I should have been more worried, but my priorities were otherwise occupied.

OLIVER

"Was that necessary?" I asked Adalynn when Abby left the room.

"What?" she replied. I didn't buy her feigned innocence. I knew it was all an act the second I looked at her face.

Ever since I had gone back to school after my father's funeral, I started to hang out with a different group of friends. Some other guys from the football team had intercepted me on my first morning back and I just continued joining them during break. They were the perfect escape from my own friends who seemed inclined to make sure I was okay, every damn second of the day. Unfortunately, Adalynn and her cheerleading squad were a part of that group. And it turned out Abby was right all along, she really was a mean person.

"I don't understand why you're always on her case, Adalynn."

"Right. Like she doesn't do the same with me."

"As a matter of fact, she doesn't. She just complains when you're shooting daggers at her."

"Well, I wouldn't be shooting daggers at her if she wasn't in the way of me getting what I want."

"What you want? What could you possibly want that you don't already have?

"That's easy. You. I've told you many times already:

I want you to be my boyfriend, Oliver. Abbygail is always in the way, she makes it impossible to get close to you."

I snickered. "Okay. First off, Abby isn't your problem in that department, Adalynn. I am not interested in dating, period. Don't take it personally. It's just not my thing. And second of all, *if* there were any chance of us being a couple, there is absolutely no way in hell I'd be dating a girl who has an issue with my best friend. She's non-negotiable."

"Then get used to being single."

"Why's that?"

"If you keep Abbygail around, there is no girl in school that will want to date you. When the both of you are together, you look like and act as if you're a couple. So between you and me, you might as well be dating her, Oliver."

"Maybe I will." The words escaped my mouth without me thinking twice about it and I walked out the patio door.

I recognized the distinct smell of his weed the moment I stepped out. Damian was sitting alone near the in-ground pool, looking at the sky and its peacefulness. I was tempted to ask him for a hit, but then changed my mind. With the amount of alcohol I had in my blood, adding drugs in the mix wasn't the best of ideas.

"Mind if I join you?" I asked him, taking the Adirondack chair beside his.

He barely gave me a glance and shrugged. I wasn't surprised or offended by his reaction though, it's just how he was. Damian didn't care about much and even less about what people thought of him. To me, the guy was our school dealer, and before my dad died, I'd never really paid attention to him. The one thing I did know, though, was that the guy was a freaking genius. The fact that he was always at the top of the class, even though he was high, aggravated the hell out of me.

Over the week I hung out with the guys on the football team, I got to know Damian a lot better than I had in five years. He was our quarterback's best friend, and although he didn't play football himself, I noticed that he knew a lot more about the sport than he let show. He always had some helpful feedback to give the guys after their practice.

I looked up at the dark sky and watched the low white moon through the branches. The sky was extremely dark and the color of the orb around the moon reminded me of Abby's deep ocean-blue eyes. I hadn't seen that color since before her mother interrupted our staring competition at school the day my dad died. Ever since then, whenever I crossed her path, her eyes were gray or pale blue, and deep down I knew it was my fault.

"How are you doing?" Damian asked, interrupting my somber thoughts.

"As good as one can be after losing his dad. You?"

He shrugged. "Better than you, I guess. Want some?"

What the hell, why not...

I stretched out reaching for his lit joint.

"What the fuck do you think you're doing?" Abbygail berated, reappearing out of nowhere. I knew I would need to face her sooner or later, but later was what I had been hoping for.

"What does it look like?" I sneered, annoyed by her sudden presence.

"Looks like you're being an idiot."

I rolled my eyes. "Just leave, Abby."

"Why?"

"What do you mean why? Because I just asked you to. Could you just please not be your exasperating self right now and go back inside the house?"

"Great. So now I'm exasperating. Go to hell, Oliver." She showed me her back and addressed Damian. "Do you have any more of that?"

"You mean the weed?" he asked, surprised.

She nodded.

She wouldn't dare, would she?

"Sure." He pulled out another joint from inside his coat.

"No," I growled, just as he stretched out to hand it to her. I knocked his arm, and the rolled-up paper hit the ground.

"What the fuck, man?"

"Abby. Inside. The. House. NOW!"

"No."

"Abbygail Evens, get the fuck out of here. You are not smoking this shit."

"Says who?"

"Says me."

"Really? Well, guess what, ass-hat? You aren't my dad. If you're going to be stupid enough to get high, then I'm going to do it with you."

I should have known.

"Freckle Face, look at me." She raised her sad eyes to mine, and I could see her pain in them. She didn't want to take the drugs, but she'd do it anyway, just because it was me. "I don't want you to do this. This isn't you."

"It isn't you either." Tears were pooling out of her eyes.

She's wrong. This is me...

"Okay, Abby you're right." I repeated the words in my head three times, to make sure they would be coming out correctly, and I took my best friend's cold hand. I looked deeply into her eyes and lied to her.

"Abbygail, I'm sorry. I won't do it. I promise. Now go back inside, and I'll join you in a minute."

She gave me a resolved nod, and walked back the way she came.

"Your girl is kind of a buzz kill," Damian commented once Abby was out of earshot.

He picked up the joint I'd made him drop on the ground and gave it to me. I took it, but I made sure she wasn't looking back when I hid it in my sweatshirt's front pocket.

"She isn't my girl."

"Really? Then you won't mind if I take her to that room upstairs and fuck her tonight?" I could feel my blood boiling, but within a matter of seconds he coughed out a loud laugh. "Dude. It's a joke. Abby's off limits. I get it."

He reached inside his backpack and handed me a bottle containing two pills.

"What is it?"

"Oxy. Think of it as a gift from me to you, for your father's passing."

"Dude I don't–"

"Keep it. Try it or don't. I really could care less. But if you like it, and want more, then let me know. I'll see what kind of deal I can cut for you."

I frowned, unsure that I liked the idea of holding such a powerful and addictive drug in my hand. Weed was one thing. OxyContin was an entirely different story.

"I'm sorry about whatever just happened before."

"Don't be, I get it. It's better to keep her off the shit anyway." He stood ready to leave. "Hey, Oliver, can I offer you a piece of advice?"

I nodded.

"If you want Abbygail to be yours, then stop playing around and make her yours. If you don't, sooner or later, someone *will* take her away from you."

ABBYGAIL

I waited for Oliver but he never came back inside. He climbed the backyard fence and left the party without looking back.

And, unfortunately for me, his disappearing act wasn't even a surprise.

CHAPTER TEN

OLIVER

I called a cab after walking out of Zoey's backyard. It picked me up at the end of the street and dropped me off at the skate park near my house. Park hours were over, but I liked sitting there alone. The quiet made my nerves relax and without the several hundred voices around me trying to make sure I was okay, I was able sit down and think.

As I crossed the fence, I took out the weed Damian gave me and lit up. After inhaling and exhaling a couple of times I made my way to my favorite ramp.

"Have any extra for me?" I heard a voice hidden in the darkness.

"Tyler?" I squinted my eyes, surprised by his unexpected presence. "Why aren't you at Zoey's party."

"Didn't feel like going."

I frowned and took a seat beside him, letting my feet dangle over the edge of the ramp just like his were. "You look like shit, man, what happened?"

It took a while for him to answer, but when he did, I heard the quake in his voice. "When I came home from school the cops were at the house. My dad beat the shit out of my mom."

I raised my eyebrow speechless. I couldn't believe what I was hearing. "Dude—"

"Don't. I don't want to talk about it."

He took the joint out of my hand and puffed in slowly. I could tell it wasn't his first time, and the thought confused me, I wasn't aware Tyler smoked pot.

"Why aren't *you* at the party?" he asked me curiously.

"I was. It sucked. I left."

"Was Abby there?"

"Of course she was."

"Then what's the problem?"

My brows furrowed. "What do you mean?"

"Well, normally when the two of you are together, you always find a way to have fun."

I snatched my weed out of his hold and put it to my lips. "Abby and I aren't on speaking terms right now."

"I noticed." He chuckled. "What happened?"

"I don't know. I just can't stand to be around her."

"I'm sorry, I don't get it. She's your best friend. Why are you not talking to her?"

"Things have been different, ever since I kissed her."

"Wait. You *kissed* Abby? When the hell did that happen?

"The day before my dad died."

"Really?"

I nodded.

"Dude, I can't believe you've kept this from us. How was it?"

I smiled, thinking about Abby's soft root beer tasting lips, but didn't respond.

"That good, huh? So, what happened after that?"

"Nothing. My dad died."

He frowned, not quite understanding my answer. "So, you two haven't talked about it?"

I shook my head.

"Did she kiss you back?"

I frowned, surprised by the question.

"What?"

"My dad asked me the same thing the morning after it happened. My kissing Abby is the reason he was late for work."

"What do you mean?"

"He was late because I was too busy thinking about how confused I was when I was supposed to get ready for school. It's the last thing we talked about, actually."

"What did he say?"

I sighed. It was hard enough to talk about the last time I had a real conversation with my father; it was even harder to face the fact that I was responsible for his death. The thought had been gnawing at me for days.

There was nothing to do. I couldn't shake off the guilt.

"He said that Abby felt for me what I felt for her and to give her time."

"And what do you think?"

"I think that if Abby was in love with me she would have told me. She isn't one to keep quiet about her feelings, so whatever he thought he knew, he was wrong."

"Have you thought about asking her?"

"Yeah, I don't think so. Besides, like I said, we aren't talking now."

"Why not? And what's with the both of you anyway?"

"I don't know. I'm just...like I said earlier, I can't stand being around her."

Silence fell between the both of us. I got lost in my own thoughts, and was surprised when Tyler stood ready to leave.

"Need to get home?"

He nodded and hopped off the ramp. "Can I ask you something?"

"Of course."

"What would you do if another guy asked Abby out?"

"Probably beat the shit out of him. Why?"

He shrugged. "It's just a question. I have to go check on my mom. Please don't tell the others about what happened."

CHAPTER ELEVEN

OLIVER

I sat high up on the bleachers overlooking the football field while my team started their warm up. The last time I set foot on the field for practice with them was during our summer try-outs, and the funny thing was that I didn't miss it. Or at least that's what I led myself to believe.

"I thought you weren't going to show up," Stephan said as he climbed up the benches to join me.

"If it makes any difference, I didn't think I would be here either."

"Coach threw a fit when he saw you weren't on the field again. He's really pissed off at you, Oliver."

"So?"

"So? He's going to kick you off the team. What's with

you? You haven't been to practice since school started. Football was your thing, and now it's like you don't care."

I laughed, and Stephan looked at me, irritated by my lack of tact.

"Want to clue me in on what's so funny?"

I shrugged and shook my head.

"You're high again, aren't you?"

"Dude, you have no idea what you're talking about."

"Really? Then maybe you should make a small trip to the bathroom and look at your stupid grin and your bloodshot eyes," he suggested angrily. "I just don't get why you do it, Oliver."

"What do you mean, why? It's just a bit of weed, Steph. It helps to take the edge off."

He shook his head, clearly not agreeing with me, but thankfully, he didn't push the subject further.

"Where's Abby?" I asked, curiously.

"She came when the bell rang and left maybe five minutes later."

"She never misses practice."

"You're right, she doesn't. *You* do. She's been coming here every day for two weeks waiting for you to show up. She probably got fed up sooner than usual and took the bus home instead."

"I could have been a few minutes late. It happens. She shouldn't have left."

"You're an idiot," he replied.

"Piss off, Stephan. She should be here."

"What the hell for? You're never here."

"I am now, aren't I?"

He looked out at the field and then back to me. "Whatever, Oliver. I'm not here to defend her. I really couldn't care less about where she is, or what she's doing. What I care about is you. Tell me what the hell is going on."

A long silence lingered between us. Stephan and I hadn't really talked in a while. When we'd hang out, it was more about him trying to distract me than getting me to talk about my feelings.

"We need to talk about the weed."

I groaned. I thought he was going to let the subject go.

"You need to quit, dude."

"Steph—"

"Shut up and listen to me. The drugs won't help, Oliver. I get it it's weed, it's not the end of the world, but in the end it's just going to make matters worse." He paused. "This isn't you."

"God." I snarled. "You sound *just like* her. How the hell would *you* know what is or isn't me?"

"Twelve years of friendship. That's how."

I put my head between my legs and pulled on my hair. I hated that he was putting me on the spot.

"I don't like it. Abby doesn't like it. She's worried sick about you."

"She sure has a way of showing it."

"She's in pain, asshole. She loved your dad, and he's gone. She loves you and—well—face it dude, you're gone too."

"Do I look like a guy that can help her? I'm a fucking screw up, Stephan. I quit everything I care for. I skip class. My grades are slipping. I take drugs, and I drink every time I get the chance."

I grabbed the bottle of pills Damian handed me at Zoey's party from inside my bag, and slammed it on the bench between Stephan and me. He took it and eyed it suspiciously.

"OxyContin." I growled. "And before you ask, no I haven't. But I've been contemplating the hell out of it... I can't be there for her Steph. I miss her. I want her. I fucking need her, but I can't have her around me because I'm going to ruin her."

Stephan opened the bottle and dropped the pills on the bench. I watched as he crushed them under his football spikes and sighed in relief.

"Thank you."

"What the hell were you thinking? If you got caught—"

"I know. Trust me." I looked up at the sky and then at him. "I'm tired, Steph. Like completely exhausted. I try to put on a strong front so that people get a fucking clue about my being okay with my life. I'm tired of everyone taking pity on me. I just want things to go back to normal."

"Dude, your dad died. You're not supposed to put up a front. Everyone knows it's going to hurt. People ask because they care and want to be sure you're okay."

"Yeah, well, it's fucking annoying."

"Things will get better."

"I don't want things to get better. I want them to disappear."

He pinched his brows as if he was trying to understand what I meant.

"I want out, Stephan. I need to leave."

"Leave?" When he realized that he understood me correctly, he looked hurt and remained quiet. The silence between us as we watched out teammates running laps was thick. "What about us?"

"We'll keep in touch. I never said I wanted to cut all ties."

"Where would you go?"

"I've been thinking B.C. You know, where my dad's family lives?"

"That's pretty fucking far, Ol."

"That's the point, Steph. No one knows me there. I can be whoever I want to be."

He sighed. "What about, Abs?"

I hadn't thought that far ahead yet, but he was

right, leaving Abby behind meant accepting the huge void I'd be inflicting upon myself. On the other hand, I had no choice.

"If I don't go, I'll drag Abby down with me." I could see him reflect on what I was trying to say.

"Dude, you're my best friend. I can't imagine all the shit that's going through your head right now, but honestly, man…" He sighed. "I don't want to see you go, Oliver."

Coach drew out his whistle, and Stephan grabbed his helmet looking at me sadly.

"I need to go." He reached the grass, and glanced up at me. "Talk to your mom, Oliver. She'll listen to you. Tell her how you feel, and then see what she thinks."

After watching the football practice and yearning to be on the field, I took the second bus service home. The drive took twenty minutes instead of the usual ten in the morning. I enjoyed the ride, though. It gave me a chance to reflect on everything Stephan and I talked about. My voicing of how much I was missing my best friend started to hit me in ways I wouldn't have imagined… or maybe it was just my afternoon high withdrawal. Who knew?

I'm wrong. I can't do this. I need her. I miss talking to her. I miss her smile; her tantrums. I miss our arguing and holding her hand, but most of all I miss my Abby.

I felt my throat tighten as I looked out the window. The last thing I wanted was to cry. I suppressed the tears that were threatening to fall and I stared ahead, watching the town and its people pass by as the bus drove me home. It had been at least three weeks since Abby and I spent some quality time together. Had she been with me, we either would have gotten off two stops ahead of ours to share a root beer slushy while we walked home, or she would have tried to race me home, claiming she was faster than I was, even though I'd beat her every time.

Ever since I left her at the hospital, I wanted to feel different about Abby, but I also wanted to protect her and the only way I could do it was by staying clear from her.

I tried to keep her away and it was hard as hell. But I knew that eventually I would become greedy and selfish. I'd be taking everything she had to offer me and would destroy both of us in the process. It's the exact reason why I couldn't stay.

She was leaning against her bedroom window when I passed her house. It was almost as if she waiting for me Her clouded eyes probably resembled my own. As I crossed the street, she waved with a tentative smile. But instead of responding, I frowned at her, wondering if she regretted not sticking around for practice.

"So what?" I heard her yell when her front door opened. "You're not even going to say hello now?"

I turned around to a very sexy-looking Abbygail standing in her doorway. She was wearing her god-forsaken dark, blue boot-cut jeans and her bright red belly button shirt. Her hair was down, and she was wearing make-up, which were two things she rarely did. I groaned.

Being attracted to your best friend like this should be illegal... God, she's hot.

While I took the time to figure out why she was all dressed up, I had this sudden surge of jealousy towards whomever she was going to spend the evening with. But what surprised me the most was all the bottled-up the anger I had towards my best friend.

"Abbygail," I warned loudly enough for her to hear. "Don't."

"Oh, I get it. I'm basically the piece of trash you just decided to discard. Sixteen fucking years of friendship, and you can't even bother to say hello? If you want our relationship to be over, Oliver, just tell me. That way I'll stop wasting energy on trying to fix something I don't even know how I broke."

It was inevitable. I dropped my bag on my lawn and crossed over to hers. Never taking my eyes away from her, I jumped over the huge rock in front of her house and leaned into her so close that even a piece of paper couldn't have passed between us.

I grabbed her by the nape of the neck, and pulled her head up to face mine. I didn't even know what my next move was. Her perfume attacked my nostrils with its sweet citrus fruit smell, and all I wanted to do was kiss her. Desire pulsing through my veins, I looked at her eyes; they changed from crystal blue to sapphire in a fraction of a second.

Sapphire? This is new...

I felt her pulse quicken against my hand and I swallowed hard. She mimicked my move, and bit her bottom lip.

"Don't do that."

"Do what?"

"Bite your lip, Abby. Stop doing it."

"Why?"

Because if you don't, I'm going to fucking kiss you, Abbygail. That's why.

"Just because."

"If you're going to be mad at me, Oliver, at least have the courtesy to tell me why."

I didn't respond. I just stared at her contemplating my next move, but most of all trying to control my urges.

I had no idea what was going on between us. I was still holding her so close to me, and for a reason I didn't understand, she was refusing to pull back. I wondered if she was trying to defy me or wanted to see how far I would take our confrontation. She wasn't scared of me, but I was. I was working very hard at controlling my impulses, but especially at keeping my temper in check. I had never lost control or got truly angry with Abby before. Whatever was going on between us was completely foreign to me. Jealousy and lust didn't make a good mix where my best friend was concerned. "I don't remember you missing a game or practice of mine for no reason."

"You don't go to practice, Oliver. But if you did, you would have seen that I made it to the field every single day for the past two weeks waiting for you to show up."

"I was there today. But then you wouldn't know that, would you?" I hummed against her skin. "Why did you come home so early today? Needed to make yourself slutty for your date tonight?"

The force of her push was unexpected. But it was the hurt I saw on her face that made me nearly lose my balance.

"Abby, I'm –"

"Don't. I don't want to hear it. I went to practice, Oliver. I went, and you didn't show up. Again. I missed the fucking bus and walked home, alone. Again. So, don't stand there and judge me, or my intentions, because of *your* lack of attendance and *your* anger towards life. I'm trying here. Seriously, Oliver, you either want me around or you don't. Figure it out and tell me."

She waited for my reply and I stood there, speechless.

"Say something, Oliver."

Silence.

"Anything," she growled.

I saw the tears fill up in her eyes as she bit the inside of her cheek to keep herself from crying. And to make matters even worse, I shrugged.

"I'm done," she relinquished. "I give up."

"I guess were done being friends, then." I stated or asked—I'm not quite sure—with spite.

She turned to me, and the tears she was trying to hold onto escaped her crystal blue eyes. "Go to hell, Oliver"

My mother was waiting for me at the door when I stepped inside our house. And having her stand there waiting for me was definitely not good news.

"Where were you?"

"I was talking with Abby. Why?"

"I meant this afternoon, Oliver."

"School. Where else should I have been? What's with you?" I frowned defensively. I was still shaken by what had happened between Abby and me. My mother's presence wasn't helping.

"How about you tone down the sarcasm and reconsider your answer."

I rolled my eyes at her. "There's nothing to reconsider, Mom."

"Okay, then let me rephrase since you clearly can't see the position you're in right now. *Rethink* your answer, Oliver."

"I don't know what you're talking about." I headed up to my room. "How about *you* butt out of my business, and trust me? Clearly *you* don't see how annoying you're being right now."

I dropped my bag on the floor and waited to see if she'd call me back before shutting the door. After hearing nothing but silence, I threw myself on my bed, grabbed my headphones, laptop, and lost myself to the sound of my music.

As I opened my messenger account, I realized I had at least ten unread messages. Scrolling through the names, I clicked on the only name I was interested in. Abby, had messaged me at three forty-five.

BlackOrchid: Oliver, I went to the field after school. You weren't there... again. I don't get it. Where are you? I miss you, Oliver. You know you can talk to me about everything, don't you? Anyway, I'm going to the movies tonight with Ava and Chris. You know that guy from school she keeps talking about? Do you want to join us? I'd really like to spend some

time with you. I feel like we haven't talked in forever. Plus, I know how much you wanted to see 'Resident Evil 3'... Let me know, okay?

I startled when my computer screen went down while reading Abby's message. Looking up, I saw my mother's furious eyes staring at me.

"Take them off," she ordered.

I followed through and took my headphones off. She leaned close to me and grabbed my chin. Pulling my face to hers, she made sure she had my undivided attention.

I cowered under her scowl.

"I'm going to start by saying that what just happened downstairs will never happen again. You do not disrespect me like that, and you do not walk out on me in the middle of a conversation, Oliver Langton. Have I made myself clear?"

I nodded, and she let go. I pulled away as far as I could from her, massaging away the pressure sensation that still lingered on my jaw. She pulled out the chair I had at my desk and sat beside my bed.

"Now that this has been cleared up, I'm going to ask you one last time. Where were you this afternoon?"

"Mom, I already told you. I was at school."

She studied me quietly with narrowed her eyes. "Do you know what I'm wondering right now?"

No, but I bet you're about to tell me.

"I'm wondering, at what point in time did you decided that lying to your mother was considered acceptable? I'm asking myself how long it will take for you to realize that I already know. And that no matter how long I have to wait—because trust me, I will—the truth will come out of your mouth."

I swallowed at her threat.

"Do you know whom I've had the pleasure of talking with this afternoon?"

I shook my head, but a teacher would have been a good guess.

"Your school principal," she scolded. "And he had some very interesting information to provide regarding your class attendance. Mind you, Oliver, I do not appreciate being called at work to be told that my son isn't in math class like he's supposed to be, and that he's also missed at least four other afternoons in the past week. I especially do not appreciate being lied to, by said son, when I asked him where he was this afternoon."

"Mom, I–"

"And then," she continued cutting me off as if my situation weren't bad enough. "When I get home, I check my voicemails and surprise, surprise, I have another message regarding my dear young boy, but this time it's from his football coach."

I winced.

"So, I listen to Mr. Collins as he explains to our machine that you haven't been to practice in weeks, that he understands that your dad died and excuses your absence for the first weeks following the try-outs, but that ever since you've been back in school, you haven't shown up on the field... not even to tell him that you're not feeling well."

"But Mom—"

"He also said that if you miss another practice without a valid excuse, you're off the freaking team, Oliver. Would you care to explain what the hell is going on *now*?"

She waited patiently as I considered what my answer should be. None of what I was concocting in my head would have her less mad at me, so I ended up shrugging in response.

"I'm waiting, Oliver."

"And I have nothing to say, Mom."

"Really? Then you can stay in your room for the rest of the evening." She stood. "We'll try this again tomorrow."

"Oh come on, I was supposed to go to the movies with Abby tonight." I didn't want to go, but if it got me out of a punishment, then why not?

"Honey," my mother responded with a sarcastic chuckle. "You haven't spent time with Abbygail since the funeral. I know this because she told me. And even if I did believe you—which, FYI, I don't—you won't be going."

"But it's true. I was just messaging her back when you walked in. See?" I lifted my laptop for her to look at, but she didn't give it a side glance.

"You can message her that you're not going," she replied as she walked out of my room.

I threw my headphones at the door as soon as she shut it behind her, but after hearing the loud thump, she reopened the door, looked at my headphones on the floor, then met my scowl.

"Just so you know, if you cut class again, you're grounded. No T.V., no videogames, no going out, no phone, and no computer for a month. Do I make myself clear?"

I glared at her, defying her authority.

"I don't think I heard your answer, Oliver."

"Yes." I grumbled.

She dipped her head in acknowledgement and shut the door quietly.

OliSk8: Can't come.
BlackOrchid: Can't or won't?
Olisk8: Both

I waited for her response.
I didn't get one.

. . .

My mother ended up never calling me for dinner. By seven thirty my stomach was growling. By ten o'clock, the night had officially settled in, and I was starving. Feeling somewhat courageous, I decided to go downstairs and prepare myself something to eat. Part of me hoped that she wouldn't hear me. I'd grab some food and make myself scarce by going back to my room. But when I got to the ground floor, I spotted a car rolling into the Evens' driveway. I stepped closer to the window and heard the loud hip hop music blasting from the pimped up red Honda Civic. I frowned, wondering who Abby could be with.

Heated rage coursed through my veins when I saw her and some guy step out of the car. She was still wearing the same clothing she had on when I saw her in the afternoon. As they spoke, his fingers were grazing her bare stomach. I couldn't even tell if she was uncomfortable with it or not, but all I wanted to do was pull him away from her. Every ounce of jealousy I had earlier resurfaced, but the intensity of it felt ten times what it was. My blood was boiling.

"Come on, Mason. Let's go." Ava shouted from the inside the car. "We need to drive Chris home."

Mason put his finger up, asking her for an extra minute, and Abby giggled. When they started talking again, Ava honked the horn a second time.

Thank God. I really need to remember to thank her Monday morning.

Abby laughed at her friend's impatience and walked back to her door. As she put her hand on the handle, Mason leaned in and left a soft kiss on the side of her mouth. From where I stood, Abby seemed surprised, but not displeased by his bold move.

My heart snapped.

My father died and it was my entire fault.

It was one simple kiss.

One moment.

One lack of judgement, and because of it—it was all over.

Because of it my best friend, the girl I loved more than life was in someone else's arms.

I knew deep down that my decision would shatter her, but at that exact moment, I didn't care.

I was done with the guilt, done with the pain.

And one way or another, my mother would agree to let me go to B.C.

CHAPTER TWELVE

OLIVER

"We need to talk," I said to my mother stepping out of the house. She was on the steps of our backyard deck stretched out, looking up at the sky with her hands settled behind her head. "Mom?"

"Huh?" She turned, surprised to see me. "Oh. I'm sorry I didn't hear you come out."

"Mom, can we talk?"

"Of course. Come sit with me. It's pretty nice out, but you really should have put a warmer shirt on, Oliver. It's a lot colder than it was this afternoon."

Her comment threw me off guard. She was acting weird, addressing me as if what had happened a few hours before never took place.

I shook my head confused. "Mom, I'm sorry. I'm

sorry about what happened earlier. I'm sorry about school, I'm sorry about everything."

I took a seat beside her, and my shoulders started to shake. I couldn't hold back anymore. My whole life was falling to pieces and going down the drain. I didn't want to cry, but the pain of everything was just too much to handle.

"Oliver." She looked into my desperate eyes. "Sweetheart, I know you miss him. I miss him too, a lot. But we need to be able to talk to each other if we want to get through this."

I nodded. She was right, but she had no idea how bad things were. My telling her was scaring the shit out of me. She wiped away the huge teardrop rolling down my cheek, and took my hand, rubbing it gently to comfort me. I was so lucky to have her. I hated the way I had been acting with her.

"What's going on in that head of yours, kid?"

Not quite ready to make a confession I inhaled and exhaled loudly.

"Oliver?"

"I want to move."

"Move?" she chuckled. "Why in world would we move?"

"Because," I replied, resolved. "I can't stay here anymore. Everything is just—I can't."

She frowned and waited patiently for me to continue.

"I screwed up. I fucking screwed up. Dad's gone. Abby hates me. My grades are slipping. I quit football. I cut class. I'm on drugs. I drink... Mom, I can't do this anymore."

"Wait. What?" She let go of my hand. "Fuck."

I winced.

"I don't even know where to start." She stood and walked around the yard in silence for a minute, and turned back to me. She was on the verge of her own tears. "Oliver?"

"I'm sorry."

"Drugs, Oliver, really?"

"It's just weed and I only smoke to take the edge off. It's just to help take my mind off things, Mom."

"So let me get this straight..." She looked up at the sky, and I was pretty sure she was mumbling every swear word she could possibly think of under her breath. "You think taking drugs and alcohol are the right solution to make things easier? For Christ sake, Oliver. Drugs, it's—I—" She frowned. "I don't get it. What's—Why? What the hell are you thinking?"

"I'm thinking—I'm thinking that I hate my life. I'm thinking that I miss my dad. I'm thinking that I'm losing my best friend because I can't stand to be around her anymore. I want the pain to go away. The drugs, they help—I don't know. They just help okay?"

"No, kid, it's not okay. It's stupid. What will happen

when the weed isn't enough, huh? You move on to something stronger?"

"No." I snapped. "I don't want it to get there. That's why I want to move. I want it to stop."

"Then just quit, Oliver. If you know that this isn't right, then stop doing it."

"You don't understand. I want to start fresh. I want a new life."

With every reply, the sound my mother's voice and mine increased. We were officially yelling at each other. The backyard light to our next-door neighbor's house, Mrs. Talia, turned on. The old lady peeked out of her patio door, and gave us a mean glare. It was past ten, the woman was right to be annoyed with us.

"Oliver," my mother subdued. "This is our home. Our life. Our family is here in Carrington. Things with Abby... they'll get better. She just misses your dad. She wants to help you, but she doesn't know how. If the both of you would just sit down and talk—"

"No. You don't get it. It's not just her. It's everything. I don't like it here anymore. It's too hard."

She sighed. "Where are we supposed to go, Oliver?"

"Vancouver."

"As in British Colombia?"

I nodded.

"Are you freaking crazy?" she shrieked.

"It's Dad's home. It's where he grew up."

"It's across the fucking country."

I winced at her harsh tone.

"I'm sorry," she rushed. "But you're not making sense, Oliver. You can't possibly believe that moving to B.C. is the solution to your problem."

"It is."

"But—"

"Mom, listen. I get it. I get that you don't want to go. I'll understand if you say no, but this is what I want. I've been thinking about it for a while, and honestly, getting out of here, it's what I need. You can even stay here and send me away to live with Uncle Jerry if you want. I'll be eighteen in a year, I—"

"I'm not living without you, Oliver. I just lost your dad. You can't ask me to let you move away. I need you." She rubbed her forehead and finally took her seat beside me. "Oliver, sweetie, I love you, and I understand where you're coming from. Losing your father like we did, it hurts. I'm hurting too. Everything I look at reminds me of your dad. But moving? It's—I don't know… It's a big step, Oliver. I just don't believe that you've really thought about leaving Carrington through and through. What about Abby? Your friends? What about school?"

"I'll start school as soon as we move there and pick up from where I left off here. As for friends, I'll just make new ones. It doesn't matter to me. It'll work," I argued.

I was hopeful. With the way she was questioning

me, it sounded like she was actually considering my suggestion.

"And Abby?" she repeated. "She's your best friend. You two have never lived apart from each other. Up until a month ago, you refused to spend the night without her. Are you sure you can just pick up and leave her behind?"

"I—" I exhaled and shut my eyes. Abby's beautiful orbs appeared from the darkness. I sighed, opened my eyes and shook off the shiver running up my spine. "I'll figure it out. Can you just think about it? Please?"

ABBYGAIL

I wasn't surprised that Oliver had declined my invitation, but it still stung. He'd been ragging about the stupid movie for months. I thought that by suggesting it, knowing very well that I hated the movie but would go just to make him happy, he would have at least considered my offer.

I was wrong.

I called Ava as soon as I received his rejection and told her she should go alone with Chris, but ten minutes later, she called back and told me I had a date.

I didn't want a date.

I wanted Oliver.

It turned out that Mason, Ava's nineteen-year-old cousin, was pretty cool. And hot. The movie sucked big time, but it didn't matter because Mason and I had a blast. I really enjoyed his company. He and I barely watched the movie. We either mocked Ava' and Chris's making out or talked, getting to know each other better. Mason wasn't Oliver, but he was a damn good replacement for the night.

"Hey, Mom, I'm home." I shouted from the door, walking in.

"Was that Ava's mother or father that just backed out of my driveway?"

Crap! I told him to put down the music.

I tossed my shoes into the closet. "Um, neither. Ava's parents weren't available, so her cousin, Mason, drove us."

"Mason, the guy that kissed you on my front porch?"

I winced.

"How old is he, Abby?"

"Nineteen," I answered waiting for the blow. My mother had strict rules about my driving around with people she didn't know.

"So, let me get this straight: you let a nineteen-year-old stranger drive you to and from the movies, without my knowledge, and then you let that same stranger kiss you in front of my house for our whole neighborhood to notice?"

I frowned. "He's not a stranger, Mom. He's Ava's cousin."

And since the kiss did happen, there is one particular person I hope saw it...

"I don't know him, Abby, so he's a stranger to me. How many times must I remind you that you can't just get into anyone's car without my knowing? The deal was that her parents were to drive you. What if something had happened?"

"You're overreacting. I'm here, and I'm safe and sound. What more do you want? Besides, Mason was sweet."

She made a disgusted face. "Of course, you'd think he was sweet. He's nineteen, and he kissed you. By the way, I won't agree with this relationship. He's too old for you."

"Relationship? Jeez, Mom, calm down. It was just a kiss. *Nothing* happened."

She breathed out a heavy sigh. "Abbygail, you know my rules. If you want to go out and enjoy your freedom, then you must respect them. Otherwise, deal with the consequences. Take this as your one and only warning."

I gave her a displeased nod and headed to my room. Although I appreciated the distraction, stepping back inside home was a harsh reality to come back to. Going out was nice. It took my mind off what had happened with Oliver after school, but unfortunately, it didn't erase the past.

From the corner of my eye, I saw Oliver's light turn on. I was almost compelled to climb out my window and knock on his door. I missed my best friend, but getting into another fight with him was more than I could handle for one day. He and I were barely on speaking terms. I was lucky if he acknowledged me, so showing up uninvited was probably not the best of ideas.

Sometimes, I felt like we never existed. After Zoey's party, things went from bad to worse. Oliver never came to our locker. I'd spend almost every recess waiting for him hoping he'd show up, he never did. He hardly hung out with Stephan and Tyler either. I knew, because more often than not I'd make a detour by their locker and ask how he was. Both would answer that they hadn't seen him, so they didn't know. The guys weren't hanging out with us girls all that much anymore either. Oliver had always been the glue that held us together and since he wasn't there anymore, the guys ended up not spending time with us very much.

I went to football practice every time he had one, but he obviously never showed up. I always followed him to the skate park, secretly admiring his skills, but I doubted he even realized I was there. If he did, he clearly didn't care enough to tell me. The whole thing sucked, and that afternoon when I saw him skip class and cross the school grounds to hide away in the woods with Damian, again, all I wanted to do was give up.

I wonder if he meant it...

Are we really not friends anymore?

The sound of my computer pulled me out of my rueful thoughts. I wondered who could be messaging me at ten thirty at night. Part of me hoped it would be Mason, I really liked him.

I was wrong. It was the *last* person I could have expected.

I smiled.

OliSk8: **How was your date?**

BlackOrchid: **It wasn't a date.**

OliSk8: **Funny, it didn't look like that from here...**

OliSk8: **Who's the guy?**

BlackOrchid: **Ava's cousin, Mason.**

OliSk8: **If it wasn't a date, why'd he kiss you?**

Good, I'm glad he saw.

BlackOrchid: **I don't know. Maybe because he likes me?**

OliSk8: **That's not how you kiss someone you like...**

BlackOrchid: **How would you know?**

BlackOrchid: What do you care, anyway? You didn't want to come.

OliSk8: Couldn't.

BlackOrchid: That's not what you said earlier.

BlackOrchid: Anyway, who cares? So some guy kissed me *shrugs* jealous much?

OliSk8: You wish. Get over yourself, Abby. Why would I be jealous that some old guy kissed you?

BlackOrchid: The fact that you noticed he was older tells me otherwise.

OliSk8: I'm not jealous, Abby.

BlackOrchid: I don't believe you, Oliver.

OliSk8: Once you see me, you will.

I rushed out of my bedroom and made my way to the front door.

"Where do you think you're going?" my mother called out from the living room.

"Oliver's."

"It's ten thirty, Abby. You're not going out."

"Come on, Mom," I whined. "Just a minute, please? I need to check on something."

I put my shoes on.

"I said no," she warned. "And I swear Abby, if you set one foot over that threshold, I'm taking your computer away for the weekend."

I shrugged. I could deal without a computer for a

few days, especially if it meant seeing Oliver's jealous face.

I opened the door.

"Hello, Abbygail," he grinned.

I think my heart just melted...

"Oliver —I—what are you doing here?"

"I came over to show you my non-jealous face."

He stared at my lips and smirked. I was unconsciously rubbing them, trying to wipe off Mason's kiss.

Smooth, Abby... really smooth.

"Hey, Aunt Jen."

"Oliver, does your mom know you're here?"

"Yeah," he winked subtly at me. "She gave me half an hour. Do you mind if I go upstairs with Abby for a few minutes?"

"Yes, I mind. I was just on the phone with your mother five minutes ago, and from what I understand, you're grounded for the weekend."

Well shit, he was telling the truth.

He threw me a knowing look.

"You're so busted," I mouthed.

He shrugged with a smirk that spoke a thousand words.

"Go home before I call her," my mother disciplined.

"'Night, Aunt Jenna."

"Goodnight, Oliver."

"Later?" he whispered. It was the only word he said before leaving the house.

I nodded with a discreet smile, but I was disappointed to see him go. "Hey, Oliver?"

"Yeah?" He had a bizarre grin as he walked backwards with his hands in his pockets.

"A simple guy doesn't check on his neighbor unless he's a little bit jealous."

He looked like he was about to reply something, but changed his mind and let out the sexiest chuckle on earth.

"Hey, Abby?" he shouted once he reached his front door.

"Yeah?"

"A neighbor always checks up on a girl if she's his best friend." He winked and disappeared behind his door.

I shook my head.

His moods swings are giving me some serious whiplash.
What the hell just happened?

I couldn't have wiped the smile off my face even if I wanted to. I was confused, but as I walked back to my room beaming like an idiot, I realized that it didn't matter. This was our first interaction in weeks. This was us being us, and in the end, if Oliver and I could find our way back to each other, that's all I could ask for.

After changing, I took a risk and looked out the

window. Oliver was standing bare chested in his bottom pjs, waiting for me. I groaned but didn't shy away from the window.

Not jealous, my ass

I bit my lip, appreciating the sight.

OliSk8: Stop biting your lip, Abby.
BlackOrchid: What's with you and my lip biting?
OliSk8: Nothing. Just stop doing it.
OliSk8: And by the way, I saw the way you were looking at me. I'm not comfortable with your objectifying me.
BlackOrchid: Objectifying you? Get over yourself, Langton. You're not even that cute.
BlackOrchid: Besides, your ass looks big is those pjs.

I pulled away from my screen and stretched out in front of the window. Oliver was still standing there, holding his laptop and raising his eyebrow at me.

OliSk8: My ass is not big!

I burst out laughing.

BlackOrchid: It is. Maybe you should think about walking to school more often.
Olisk8: Is that you trying to be funny?
BlackOrchid: No. That's me being funny.

OliSk8: Hey Abs?
BlackOrchid: What?
Olisk8: You do realize that you just said I was cute.

I looked back outside and shook my head but all I wanted to do was nod. My computer interrupted my gawking, and my eyes went back to the screen.

OliSk8: 'Night, Beautiful. Xxx
BlackOrchid: 'Night, Oliver.

OLIVER

"Oliver?"

"If you're moaning my name in your sleep, we're going to have serious issues, Abby."

"I'm not moaning your name, you idiot, you're hogging all the covers."

"That's because your ass is hogging all the space."

She lifted her head from off the pillow and checked the time. "It's one thirty in the morning, Oliver Langton. Don't you dare tell me my ass is big at this time of night; otherwise, *your ass* will end up on the fucking floor."

I chuckled.

"What took you so long, anyway?"

We both knew her question held different meanings, yet my silence didn't bother her. I settled myself on her pillow, and she pulled my arms around her body.

"It's about time." She yawned, and was already falling back asleep. "I missed you, Monkey Butt."

"I know. I'm sorry."

"Please don't disappear on me like that again. My heart can't handle not having you in my life."

I froze, thinking about the conversation my mother and I had after Abby came back from her night out.

I should just tell her... I know she'd understand.

But Mom hasn't said yes yet, so maybe I should just wait. Yeah, I'll just wait...

"I love you, Freckle Face."

"I love you too, Oliver." The corner of my lip curled at the sound of her lazy mumble.

CHAPTER THIRTEEN

ABBYGAIL

Something was wrong. I could feel it. Oliver and I had been back to our somewhat normal relationship, but the whole thing lasted only a few days. Now he wasn't just distant with me, it was with every one of our closest friends, as well.

"Ready to go?" Kylie asked, looking at our reflection in my bedroom mirror. The beautiful poppy and pink dress she was wearing fit her so well.

"Just about. I need to put the finishing touches on my make-up."

"What make-up? Everything you put on is so light that we can barely see you're wearing any."

"It's called sheer for a reason, Kylie. I just want the

shine, not the full-on color." I put on a layer of bubble gum lip gloss. "I'm done."

I spun on my heels and my simple short white lace dress lifted, twirling as I moved.

"Wow. Now lose the tan boots."

I rolled my eyes. "It's either these boots or my Converse shoes, Ky. Take your pick."

"Fine. Keep the boots."

"I knew I'd find a way to make you agree with me. Now tell me, how do I look?"

She smiled. "Beautiful. Any guy would be crazy to not be in awe of you tonight."

It was our homecoming dance, and since the warm fall weather had come later than usual, the committee decided to make our night a summer-themed party. Kylie and I had spent the day soaking up as much sun as we could. We went apple picking in the morning, and in the afternoon, she and I went to the skate park and spied on the guys while they were skateboarding. Fall had always been my favorite season, and the warm days we were having made it even better.

"Yeah, well, I'm not looking for any guys' attention. Just the one."

"I know. And don't worry, Abs, once he sees you, he'll go nuts. Now let's go. I don't want to be late."

. . .

"Hey." Tyler said to me as I made my way to the refreshment kiosk.

I had just spent an hour dancing with the girls and my feet were killing me.

I should have just gone with the converse shoes.

"Hey, yourself. Where have you guys been?"

"Watching you girls dance," he smirked. "You look gorgeous by the way. Like an angel in a sexy white dress."

"An angel?" I chuckled. Tyler had never been a really expressive person, and his comment had taken me off guard.

"I'm serious, Abs. I must have heard every guy in school talking about you tonight."

"Funny. Especially considering none of them approached me," I remarked.

"That's because we can't."

We?

"Can't?" I asked crossing my arms over my chest. "That's the most ridiculous thing I've ever heard, Tyler Parker."

But I could tell by the look on his face that he was serious.

"Why?"

"The question you should ask is: Who?"

I followed his gaze to the dance floor until it landed on my worst enemy's hands all over the one person I had been waiting to see all night.

"Oliver?" I frowned. I saw Tyler's nod from the corner of my eye.

I'm going to kill him.

"Come dance with me," I pleaded Tyler.

"Fuck no." The look I gave him showed how insulted I was, but I needed to hand it to him, he recovered himself quickly. "Abs, seriously do not take this the wrong way, I'd love to dance with you. But I love my balls more."

So much for your smooth come-back.

I wrinkled my nose in disgust.

"Cute." He laughed. "I'm sorry, Abby, bros before–"

I put my finger in his face. "Don't finish that sentence, or I swear to God, I'll punch you in the balls myself."

"Please don't," he begged. "Trust me, Abs, my not dancing with you is only because I promised him I wouldn't."

"So what you're basically telling me is that I'm just supposed to stand here and let him keep every guy from school away from me while he dances with Pompom Bitch?"

"Abby, I'm–"

"Don't apologize," I retorted, walking away from him. "Try growing a pair."

I couldn't believe Oliver. I mean, I understood his desire to shelter me from heart-break; it's what he had been doing for years. His protectiveness wasn't new to me. I didn't agree with it, but I never bothered telling him since he was the only guy I was interested in. His prohibition of me dancing with a friend on the other hand, well, that went a little too far.

Angry at everyone, I left the gym, and slipped inside the girl's changing rooms. There was a 'no entry' sign at the door for the night. The school committee didn't want couples disappearing inside the locker rooms, making irresponsible decisions.

The school committee needed to learn that locking doors was way more effective than a stupid sign...

"Abs?" Kylie called as soon as the locker room door shut behind her. I knew it was closed because of the double thump it made once it hit the frame.

"What?" I grumbled from behind the shower stall I was hiding in.

"You do know that you're not supposed to be here right?"

I opened the curtain and raised my eyebrow at her. Her response was to look back at me with the same annoyed look.

"You've been gone for a half an hour, Abbygail. I was worried."

"How did you know where to find me?"

She smiled and walked over to take me in for a

hug. "Because this is the secret spot where girls come to cry and find amazing friends."

I returned her smile, remembering how she and I had met at this exact same spot. But my smile faded away quickly as the thought of my best friend swooped back in and made me frown.

I wish my relationship with him could be as easy as it is with Kylie.

It was. You know, right up until you decided you were in love with him...

"Are you going to be okay?" she asked, concerned.

"I'll be fine. What's a homecoming dance without girl drama?" I asked blandly.

"An urban legend." She hooked her arm with mine and chuckled at her own lame joke. "Come on, drama queen, let's just get out of here and hit the dance floor."

We walked out from the girl's gym changing rooms and heard them talking before rounding the corner.

"You're supposed to be her best friend, Oliver," Stephan complained.

"I am her best friend."

"Well, you're not acting like one. It's like you're doing everything to purposefully hurt her."

I pulled Kylie to my side, and put my finger to my lip so I could listen.

"That's a load of bullshit and you know it."

"You're flaunting yourself in front of her with the only girl in school she despises, Ol."

"I'm just having fun, Steph. Give me a fucking break."

"You're allowed to have fun, but she isn't?" Tyler questioned.

"She's dancing with the girls, isn't she? I mean that's got to count for something."

"You're an idiot," Tyler accused. "What's with you keeping every guy in school away from her, anyway?"

"She's mine to protect."

"Dude, you are so full of shit it's beyond ridiculous. Abby doesn't need your protection. She can take care of herself."

"You're entitled to your opinion, Tyler, but I'm not changing the rule."

Rule? There's a fucking rule?

"Anyway, it doesn't matter. My relationship issues with Abby are not why I asked you here. There's something I've wanted to tell you guys for a while now."

I frowned.

"Steph, I spoke with my mom. I'm leaving."

Leaving? Already?

"What the hell do you mean you're leaving? Like on a trip or something?" Tyler seemed as confused as I was.

Oh! I hadn't thought about a trip. Wait. Why would he go on a trip and not tell me?

143

"No," Stephan answered with a sad tone. "He's moving."

Moving?

"Yeah... I'm moving to Vancouver. My Uncle Jerry is in town, and we're flying back to B.C. together on Sunday."

Sunday? As in, the day after tomorrow Sunday?

I must have heard him wrong.

"Holy shit." Kylie muttered. "That's in two days."

My head began to spin.

My heart stopped.

My world shifted.

The ache was relentless, and the one person that could truly know how excruciatingly raw it felt, was the one harshly slashing the already deep, opened wound.

CHAPTER FOURTEEN

ABBYGAIL

I tried to retain the tears, but I was clearly bad at it. In my defence, though, the sappy music playing in the background wasn't helping. Our school DJ was on a roll with his second song about love. The objective was probably to fulfil the happy couples' need to get close, but my tears and I were more than ready to move on.

I yearned for Eminem's angry lyrics. They would have satisfied those needs greatly.

"Want to dance?"

I looked up to see Tyler extending his right hand to me. I had been hiding alone, picking at my black nail polish under the gym's bleachers for quite a while, and I wondered how long it would take for one of them to find me. I wasn't expecting Tyler to be the one that would catch sight of me first.

"Please?" he begged.

I frowned. I had *the* perfect witty reply at the tip of my tongue, but he cut me off before I could say anything.

"About a half hour ago I realized that my balls were pretty big already, and that if they grew anymore my pants would rip."

I unexpectedly exploded into laughter. It was the most perfect thing he could have said, ever.

"Is that a yes?" he asked, exposing his friendly grin

I nodded and he helped me up.

OLIVER

"Told you," Damian mumbled next to me when I stepped back inside the gym. Stephan and I had been outside talking for a while after Tyler left us furious with the news I'd shared.

"Told me about what?" My brows furrowed at his nonsense, but then figured that he was probably high.

"Abbygail. I guess someone did beat you to it after all." I lifted my eyes and I saw them dancing. The sound of the melody playing got lost as I observed them closely together. She had her hands around his neck, and his hands were resting just above her ass.

I was ready to explode.

"Relax," Stephan said, standing beside me. "He's our friend, Oliver."

I swallowed the angry lump I had in my throat. Friend or not, he wasn't supposed to be dancing with her.

"Oliver," he warned. He put his hand on my arm to hold me back.

My jaw twitched and I glared at him. I had no intention of hurting Tyler, but he was definitely going to take his hands off *my* girl. "Let me go, Steph."

"Only once you've calm down."

"He isn't supposed to be dancing with her, she's mine."

There was absolutely no chance that she could have heard me, but as soon as the word escaped my lips, she lifted her head off Tyler's shoulder and stared at me. Abbygail's beauty that night hadn't ceased to amaze me. I had secretly watched her in her short white dress dancing all evening. She was carefree and completely clueless as to the number of guys watching and wanting her. Me, not as much.

How the hell am I going to protect you now? I'm not even gone yet, and there you are, already in the arms of another guy.

"Ol?" Stephan interrupted my thoughts. "You need

to tell her about B.C. before someone else does. You know how fast this shit is going to get out."

He was right. I shook off my anger and walked, crossing the entire dance floor to join the both of them. "We need to talk."

Abby looked up to me and rested her head back on Tyler's shoulder, ignoring my request.

"Abbygail."

"I'm busy."

"Yeah, that's not going to work for me, beautiful." I took her from Tyler's arms

"Oliver." she shrieked. I hauled her over my shoulder and walked back across the gym's dance floor. She kicked and screamed, and I couldn't help but smile. "Oliver, you jackass, let me go."

I settled her on the floor once we stepped away from prying eyes.

"Did you just call me a jackass?" As soon as I released my hold on her, she slipped away and busted inside the girl's locker room.

As if that's going to stop me...

The look she gave when she realized that I'd followed her inside, told me she wasn't expecting me. "Leave me alone, Oliver."

"I want to talk to you."

"And I don't. Leave." She stood still and crossed her arms, threatening me with her angry stare. "I'll scream."

"Please," I mocked. "As if someone could hear you."

"This is the girl's locker room. You aren't supposed to be in here," she argued.

"Well, the sign at the door says you aren't supposed to be in here either, Freckle Face. Besides, when has a girly logo at any door ever stopped me from following you somewhere?"

Her eyes got teary and she turned around. I frowned, not understanding where her sudden tears came from.

"What's wrong, Abs?

"Nothing," she cried. "Just leave, Oliver."

I stepped in front of her. "Abbygail Evens, I am not leaving until *we talk*."

Surprised by my tone, she glanced up. "When did you become such an overbearing jackass?"

"When have you started dancing with Tyler instead of me?"

"Right around the time you decided to—" Her eyes hit the floor. When they rose back to mine the expression on her face changed. The sadness switched to enmity in a matter of seconds.

"I decided to what?"

"Nothing."

"Abby."

"Oliver," she challenged. "I want you to fucking leave me alone."

Her angered tone only fueled mine and I had no

intention of leaving. I stepped forward, moving even closer to her, cornering her in so that she had nowhere else to go.

The feeling bubbling inside me felt like it did when I came back from the football practice she hadn't attended, the day she challenged me about our friendship, the day she showed up all dressed up and looking sexy for someone that wasn't me... except that, unlike our last confrontation, my senses weren't fuzzy. In fact, everything I was feeling for my best friend was heightened, and my desire for her felt ten times stronger than it did before.

I took another step and she took two back. We played the game until her back hit the lockers and had nowhere else to go. I advanced one last step and as soon as her eyes met mine, something changed. They went from crystal blue, to sapphire. I still had no idea what the color meant but I loved it. Her eyes lingered down to my lips and then back to meet my gaze. I wondered what was going through her mind.

She bit her bubble gum smelling lips and my heart sped up. "I thought I told you to stop biting your lip like that."

She stopped, replacing her teeth by her sweet tongue, massaging the very spot she was biting into. She just made it worse. I picked her up and pinned her against the wall, the lockers behind her rattling loudly. If we weren't careful, we would get caught.

I hadn't expected her to wrap her arms and legs tightly around me. I felt her chest rise up and down unsteadily against mine. I breathed the smell of her citrus perfume that I loved so much, and I watched as she swallowed and bit down on her lip once again.

Who gives a fuck? I'm done being careful.

I caved. I put my lips to hers, and finally let myself possess what I had been yearning for. At first, it was sweet and unsure, but I lost control. The kiss quickly transformed into a demanding need. I pulled us down to the bench behind me and straddled her over my body, losing myself in every stroke of her tongue and every graze of her teeth against my jaw and lips. She never moved away, never questioned. She just kissed me. Like she wanted it. Like she needed me just as much as I needed her.

The sound of Kylie's voice pulled us out of our embrace. "Abby?" Are you in here?"

Neither one of us said a word. We sat motionless, stared into each other's eyes, and held our breath, waiting for our intruder to go back to where she came.

I recognized the sound of 'Be the One' by The Fray playing in the background. I was tempted to tell Abby to listen to the lyrics, but as soon as the door shut behind Kylie, the silence between us became thick, and the reality of what I was doing hit me. I started to her push away, but then she tightened her grip, pressing me closer into her, and my need for the girl I was holding grew deeper.

I caressed her body and moaned under the pleasure of hers moving with mine.

"Oliver," she panted. And just as if it hit me in the face, the guilt won me over. I tore my lips away from the crook of her neck.

"Abby, we need to stop." I leaned my forehead against hers, breathing heavily but still holding her body close to mine. I said the first thing that came to mind. "I'm sorry. I–I shouldn't have kissed you."

"Okay." She frowned and touched her bruised mouth.

Leaning away from me, she eyed me suspiciously. It was almost as if she was trying to figure out if I really was regretting what had just happened between us. I didn't. I wanted more. But I also needed to explain myself. I needed to tell her everything so she could understand.

"Freckle Face, there's something I need to tell you."

I looked up to meet her eyes, but she wasn't looking at me, she was staring at our joined hands. A huge teardrop rolled down her reddened cheeks. After a moment of heartbreaking silence, she lifted her pale blue eyes to mine. "Are you really leaving?"

Wait. What? She knew?

"He told you?" I asked, fury bleeding into my tone.

"Who's he?"

"Tyler."

She shook her head. "I heard you telling them before me. It's nice to know where your true loyalty stands, though."

"That's not what it is…"

"Right." She pushed herself off me. I suddenly felt cold and empty without her.

"Abs, can we—can't we talk about this?"

"No. We can't." She backed away from me and walked out from the locker room without looking back.

"Abbygail," I yelled opening the door. Her face was wet with tears when she stopped and turned around to look at me. In the moment of silence, I pleaded her to listen to the song.

"Have a nice fucking life in B.C., Oliver."

CHAPTER FIFTEEN

OLIVER

I was shooting hoops in my front yard using my basketball as a magic eight ball when I felt her walking behind me. It was a pretty stupid game. I'd ask a question, if I got it in, the answer would be a yes. If I missed, then the answer was no. I knew that relying on a ball and basket for my answers was ridiculous, but I always experienced a sense of relief when I scored and got the answer I wanted. And at that exact moment, I needed the reassurance that everything was going to be okay.

I still couldn't believe that my mother agreed to our moving. It took her three days to decide, but I managed to convince her. When we spoke a few days after our first talk, she admitted to her struggling with my father's death. She confessed that just like me, she'd had a hard time with living in our family home and that a change of scenery could be beneficial for the both of us.

I was officially moving to B.C.

I just wasn't expecting for things to move on as fast as they did.

My Uncle Jerry, my father's brother, was a real-estate agent and my mother contacted him as soon as she gave me the news. In less than a week they had everything planned out, and I was told to pack my bags. While my mother was to stay behind to put everything in order, I was expected at Clover High, my new school, as of the following Monday.

Truthfully, with everything being so precipitated, I was starting to question my mother's motives. Obviously I wouldn't ask; the last thing I needed was for her to change her mind or question mine, but in truth it was going way too fast and I hated it. What happened between Abby and me at homecoming was confusing me about B.C., and I was starting to regret my decision to move away, completely.

Will Abby ever forgive me for not telling her I was leaving? Nah, scratch that. Will Abby ever forgive me?

"It's going to be a no." I heard her voice from behind.

I spun on my heels to face her. She was standing in my driveway in her tight ripped jeans, and her god-forsaken Rolling Stones tank top that made me lust after her body every time she wore it. She had it on so often it was all worn out.

Does she not know that I can totally see her bra through her shirt right now?

I ignored her and faced the basket. "You don't even know what I asked."

"Doesn't matter. I know you'll miss."

I did a jump shot and waited for the 'swish' sound, but it never came. The ball bounced back so hard on the backboard, it flew right into her hands.

"Told you," she jeered. She placed the ball on her hip as if she was owning a game she wasn't even playing. "And I'm ready to talk now."

"There's nothing to talk about, Abby. The decision's been made already." I extended my hand for her to give it back to me. She just glared back, not giving a shit about what I wanted. "Could you just give me the ball back, please?"

"This one?" she asked and threw it all the way across the street. How she could always find the easiest way to annoy me was beyond me.

"Really? What the hell was that for?"

"You promised you wouldn't leave me."

"I never promised anything. You asked me to never disappear on you, and I never replied."

"You knew you were leaving two weeks ago and didn't tell me?" she scorned.

"I had just spoken with my mom two weeks ago. She gave me her answer a few days later."

"I can't believe you. So that's it? You're just giving up?"

"Giving up? Abby, I lost my dad. You can't possibly know how this feels."

"News flash, Oliver, I lost my dad, too."

"Abs, your dad picked up and left on his own accord. Your situation is completely different than mine. So don't even try to compare."

"I loved your dad just as much as you did," she responded angrily.

"Maybe, but he was *my* dad." *Talk about being possessive.* "It's my fault he died, and unlike yours, there is absolutely no chance for me to see him, ever again."

"First off, my dad's a dick. I *don't* want to see him again. And secondly, how can his death possibly be your fault? You were at school when it happened, Oliver. What did you do? Call upon the car gods and pay them off so that your dad would get into an accident?"

"Stop being stupid, Abby."

"You're the one who's being stupid, Oliver. But just for the hell of it, humor me. Explain how you can possibly be responsible for a car accident that you were not a part of?"

"He was late, Abby. He was late because of me. I

kissed you, and I was worried that I had screwed up everything between us."

"If you're going to blame his death on kissing me, then I'm just as guilty as you are, because I kissed you back."

So, you did kiss me back...

Wait—no—ugh, why do I even care about this now?

I shook my head at how easily I could lose my focus when Abby was around.

"Don't be ridiculous," I muttered.

"You're the one that's being ridiculous. Your dad's death was an accident, Oliver. It had nothing to do with our kissing." Tears were forming in her crystal blue eyes. "Don't taint our kiss with your stupidity."

"Taint?"

"Yes taint. Taint as in ruin something that felt—" She pressed her lips together, silencing her next words.

"That felt what?"

Her brows pulled together as if she was trying to figure out what the appropriate answer should be. "Why did you kiss me?"

"What do you mean why?"

"It's not a college level question, Ol. You said you thought you screwed up our relationship after kissing me. Why did you do it if you were so afraid of my reaction?"

"I wasn't afraid of your reaction. I did it to piss you off, to get a rise out of you, and it worked."

"Did it?"

"Of course, it did. Don't you remember what happened when I picked you up for school the next morning?"

"Fine," she growled. If we weren't in the middle of a life changing fight, I would have been gloating. Abby finally conceding and letting me winning an argument was as rare as unicorn shit. She rubbed her temples. "What about yesterday?"

"What *about* yesterday?"

"You kissed me for like an hour in the locker room."

"Well you didn't exactly pull away now, did you?"

"I never said I did... but I'm trying to figure you out, Oliver. Did you smoke so much weed last night that you lost your line of judgement?"

I glared at her. It bugged me that she thought so little of me or us for that matter. "I wasn't high last night, Abby."

"Well, then tell me, why did we kiss yesterday?

"What do you want me to say?"

"Say *something*. ANYTHING."

"I don't know, Abbygail. I can't tell you what you want to know because I don't know. I wanted to know what it would feel like to—DAMN IT. I don't know. But it doesn't change anything."

"You're wrong. Our kissing; it changed everything. If you want to know something, then ask me. If you want to tell me something, then tell me."

"What's done is done, Abby. Just let it be."

"I CAN'T. That's what you don't get, Oliver. I'm losing you… I already lost you. I'm trying to wrap my head around what the hell is going on between us, but I can't because you won't talk to me. It's as if all of a sudden, you don't care about me—about us —anymore"

I looked away. If she didn't stop asking me all these questions, I was going to break. I didn't want her to find out how I felt about her because it would make leaving her even more difficult than it already was.

"Do not look away from me, Oliver Langton. I'm talking to you. I want you to feel exactly what I'm feeling."

Trust me, I am, and more.

"I want you to know how much you're hurting me, because all you've been doing for *weeks* is avoid me. But mostly I want you to know how much I love you, and how much you mean to me. I can't not have you in my life, Oliver. You and I, we're supposed to be a team. I need you to—I need you to breathe. My last month has been hell without you. Nothing makes sense if you're not here with me."

"You'll figure it out."

"I *don't want* to figure it out."

I let my head drop in defeat and stared at the fading daisy flowerbed Abby was standing by. The one she planted with my father for my mother's birthday last summer. The one she was digging into when I realized I was in love with her. It seemed like ages ago.

What happened?

"What happened to us, Oliver?"

"What are you talking about?"

"What happened at the hospital? What have I done, to make you hate me so much?"

"I don't hate you," I vindicated.

"Then tell me what I did wrong. I must be pretty stupid because I can't seem to figure it out."

"Abby, you are not stupid. I don't hate you, and you did nothing wrong. I—" I stopped myself from talking. I couldn't go there. Not now, not ever.

She looked at me expectantly. "You what?"

"Nothing," I bit back.

"You gave me a week. One teeny weenie week of a somewhat friendship since you shut me out at the hospital a month and a half ago. What have I done that's so horrible? But most of all, what can I do to fix it?

"There's nothing to fix, *Abby.*"

"Then tell me what to do, *Oliver*. I want you to stay. I need you."

"I want to leave, Abs. Everything here—everything I look at, it hurts. I miss him."

"And your solution is to just leave? Why?"

"Yes. Because it's just better this way."

"Better for whom? You?"

"YES, ME. My mom, me… it's better for *you*, Abby."

"This isn't better for me. I need *you*, Oliver. You're all I have left."

"Abbygail, I want you to listen to me." I took her face in my hands, bored her clear blue eyes into mine and lied. "You need to understand that I am not going to change my mind about this. I don't care what you say, or what you think you can say in hopes of changing my mind; it's not going to work. I want you to stop. And if you have ever cared for me, ever, you'll just let me go."

"Oliver I—" she frowned "—I just…"

She looked at the ground, then up to me, studying my face as she searched for or tried to figure out what she could say next. Tears clouded her beautiful face with every step she took away from me. She backed away until she reached the dying flowerbed, and when she did, she crumbled to the ground. I watched her gasp with pain, barely able to breathe. Her world was shattering, and I did nothing but watch her fall to pieces.

"Oliver, please." She wasn't looking at me, she was staring at the dead flowers before her. "You can't leave. I don't want you to go."

Maintaining silence was hard, and when she

realized that I wouldn't respond to her pleas she looked up to me, and I shook my head. The loud cry she let out wrecked me. I was coming to terms with leaving the girl I loved behind, but abandoning and purposefully hurting my best friend was an entirely different story.

Even if it was for her own good, my heart was breaking right along with Abbygail's.

I wasn't even gone and I already missed her.

She picked herself up from the ground before I shut the door. I watched her stand, in hopes of seeing her walk away from us. If it was easy for her to get up and leave, then it would be easier for me to say goodbye.

But I was wrong.

When I saw her rise unsteadily, I realized that her pain was sufficient enough for me to change my mind.

The second she looked up at me, I begged her with my eyes. It was as if everything had been forgotten, and that all I wanted was for her to say something, to ask me to stay one last time. If she did, I would ask my mom to call everything off. I knew that I was being selfish, but I didn't want to be without Abby anymore. She was right, she and I, we were a team.

"Oliver," she blubbered.

I held her gaze, showing her that I was there, that I needed her just as much as she needed me, that all she had to do was ask me to stay home, and I would.

But there was something wrong.

Something in her dark eyes told me that it was too late; they were void of tears but filled with pain.

"I hate you."

And the worst part of her words; what had siphoned the last light of my broken soul was that for the first time in our lives, she meant it.

CHAPTER SIXTEEN

OLIVER

"Seems to me like you're in need of a talk with our next-door neighbor," my mother said, taking me out of my slumber. I looked up to her standing in the doorway of my dark room.

After my argument with Abby, I called Damian, got my fix and came back home to an empty house.

"What time is it?" I asked, eyes still adjusting to the light.

"Almost eight p.m."

Great, I managed to sleep all day. Damian Bushmans you're a fucking genius.

"I'm hungry. Did you prepare anything for dinner?"

Her eyes narrowed. "There's some left-over roast-beef from yesterday in the fridge. You can make

167

yourself a sandwich. We were supposed to have dinner with the Evens' tonight. Remember?"

I racked my brain, trying to recall when I had agreed to have dinner at Abbygail's house, but couldn't figure it out.

"She wasn't up for it either. So don't feel bad."

"Trust me, I don't."

"Okay..." She frowned. "So now I'm really curious. What happened between the both of you today?"

"She found out I was leaving tomorrow."

"Just now?" my mother shouted. Her harsh voice made me flinch, although it might also have been the fact that she was just very loud, and I wasn't quite awake yet. "How could you keep information like this from your best friend, Oliver? What the hell is the matter with you?"

Nope, that was her being mad, after all.

"I kept it from everyone, not just her, and she found out yesterday. Today we just had a really bad fight about it."

"I doubt an extra fifteen hours makes much of a difference in her opinion, kid." She crossed her arms over her chest and glared at me. "And honestly, I'm going to side with her on this one."

I rose from my bed and flattened my messy hair with my Volcom cap on. "I don't see what the problem is."

"How about trying to reverse the roles, and stand in her shoes for a sec?"

Okay, let me rephrase: You don't see what the problem is.

"How would you feel if your best friend upped and left within hours of notifying you?"

How would you feel if you needed to stand in front of your best friend, with whom you are also in love, and tell her that you want to change your entire life because you're not worthy of her or anything else in life?

"You don't get it."

"You're right. I don't. She's your best friend, Oliver. She's our family."

"Mom, I made this decision for myself. It was just better for me this way. If you wanted her to know before now, you should have just told her yourself two weeks ago, when you told me."

"Trust me, I wanted to, but her mom and I agreed that the news should come from you, seeing as you're the one who made the request to move in the first place."

"I bet you were just hoping I'd change my mind."

Her lips pursed and that's when I understood why she'd planned my leaving as quickly as she did.

I slipped on my hoodie, and crossed my arms over my chest. "Well, I'm not. Your plan backfired, Mom. We're moving. Living here, with Dad gone, it's too much to handle."

"And what about, Abby?"

"What about her?" I slipped passed my mother, and went down the steps.

"You two have been inseparable for sixteen years."

"She'll figure it out," I retorted, stepping inside the kitchen. I reached inside the fridge, and looked for the ingredients to make myself a sandwich.

I would have preferred pizza, but whatever.

"Will she? And what about you? How will you deal with your feelings for her?"

I dropped a lump of mayo on my bread and glanced up at my mother. I studied her face and tried to figure out if she really knew that I was in love with my best friend, or if she was just insinuating. I opted for number two, and returned to my sandwich making.

"I have no feelings for Abbygail."

"Seriously?"

"Yes, Mom, seriously. Now could you please just butt out? I'm tired of talking about this."

"You can't leave her like this, Oliver. If you do, it will destroy her. It will destroy you."

"Fine." I muttered with my mouth full. "I'll finish this and then I'll go see her."

It was cold when I stepped outside. The dark sky was filled with imposing clouds, and I shivered under their darkness. There was something about the light of the moon and the stars hiding behind their shadows that felt unsettling. My mother had all but kicked me out of the house, complaining about my procrastination and delaying the inevitable. She understood nothing. It took me a little over two hours to summon up my courage to go see my best friend. I kept trying to decide if leaving while Abby was mad at me was better than us making peace. If she was mad at me, then maybe she would miss me less, and if she missed me less, then maybe I could pretend like I didn't care... but the truth was, I did care. I would always care.

I crossed the street to climb up my best friend's bedroom window, but hit a dead end. Her keeping me from coming inside was the last thing I would have ever expected. When I climbed back down, I was completely demolished.

"Oliver?" Aunt Jenna questioned, answering her front door.

I tried to keep my composure but it was useless. Never in eight years had Abbygail locked her bedroom window. I broke. "She locked me out."

Jenna looked at me sadly and took me into a motherly hug. "She's outback, sitting under the willow tree. She's refusing to come back inside. Go talk to her, Oliver. Please."

From the deck I saw Abby lying on a blanket. She was wearing my old football jersey and holding the big stuffed teddy bear I had won for her at the fair during that same summer. She was sleeping. I wanted to wake her up. I wanted to scream and shout at her. She had no idea how locking her bedroom window shattered me. But then I joined her under the tree, and took one look at her—her reddened wet cheeks, her puffy eyes, all the tears she had let flow—and I couldn't do it.

"If I could take your pain away," I whispered, taking a seat beside her. "I would."

The occasional rustling of the remaining leaves interrupted the quiet and made her shiver, but she didn't wake. When a gust of wind passed through the almost bare branches, I unfolded the comforter I had brought from inside and laid it gently over her small frame. Every night, since I learned that I was moving away, I'd climb up to Abby's room without her knowing and sit by her side, absorbing as much of her beauty as I could. I sat there for hours, took her hand and watch my beautiful best friend sleep, forced myself to remember every detail of her perfect face, and my last night with her was no different.

I imagined my life without her and I couldn't help asking myself if maybe my mother was right. I thought about Abby and how hard life would be if I didn't have her by my side. My selfish desires were starting to win over; she and I had gone through so much over the years…

Why would now be any different?

And that's when it hit me.

'You're my best friend Oliver. I'll do everything with you and I'd do anything for you'

It was one simple conversation, but her words meant a lot more than she could have possibly imagined. I knew my best friend. My pain would become hers. My decisions would become hers and my drowning, would mean losing her in the same way. I may have been struggling with my decision to leave, but I would never struggle with my need to protect her.

I stood and I left the Evens' backyard without looking back, and when I clipped that padlock, I let the remainder of my unshed tears fall.

CHAPTER SEVENTEEN

OLIVER

I had cut my last night of rest in Carrington way too short, so it felt way too early when I heard the doorbell ring. My mother called my name at least twice before making it upstairs to get me, but my legs didn't want to follow my will to stand up. I was exhausted. The couple of hours I had spent alone in the skate park after watching Abby sleep might have been too excessive, but it was the only way I found to remain sober.

"Oliver?" My mother knocked softly on my bedroom door. "You have a visitor."

I looked at the time.

Who could possibly be visiting me at seven thirty in the morning? Maybe it's Abby... Please let it be Abby.

"Yeah, Mom, just give me a sec." I got dressed and opened the door.

"What time did you get in last night?"

I shrugged. "I don't know. Why?"

"Did you get high again? Wasn't yesterday afternoon enough for you?"

How the hell did she figure that out?

She wasn't even here...

"I didn't get high yesterday, Mom. I went to the skate park and worked on my ollie all night. Why are you accusing me, anyway?"

"Because you look like shit, Oliver."

I rolled my eyes. "Whatever. Who's at the door?"

"Stephan."

"Oh." I frowned, but recuperated quickly under her questioning gaze. "Okay, cool."

"You didn't patch things up with Abby last night, did you?" Unfortunately, it seemed that my mother had caught my mishap.

I scratched the itch on my jaw. "Of course, I did. She and I are great. Is Steph outside?"

"Yes," she replied, distrustful of my hurried answer. "He didn't want to come in."

I scurried downstairs ignoring her piercing gaze and opened the door to a gloomy Stephan sitting on the white steps of my front porch.

"Steph."

He turned to me, giving me a sad smile. "Hey. Whoa. You look like shit. Did I wake you up?"

I nodded. "What's up?"

"Just out for a run. I figured since I was in the area I'd stop by before you left."

"In the area? I can't believe you just jogged across town."

He raised his shoulder in defeat. My leaving was affecting him a lot more that I would have expected.

"I'm sorry." It was the only answer I could sum up.

"It's just–I don't get it. I know we talked about this yesterday, but it's fucking fast, Oliver. Like… how could you just tell your mother about this two weeks ago and already be ready to leave? Your house isn't even up for sale yet."

"I told you, I'm leaving with my Uncle Jerry." I sighed. 'He came down from B.C. to help my mom with all the house stuff, you know, him being a real-estate agent and all, and she told me to pack my bags. She'll be staying here a couple more weeks to make sure everything is in order and to pack. When our new house is ready, she'll join me in B.C. If our home isn't sold by then, Abby's mom will take care of following everything through."

"Why don't you just move with your mother in a couple of weeks then?"

I felt the warmth of the sunlight trying to pierce through the massive clouds, but they didn't manage to stay long enough. The cool wind blowing the dark clouds back together made me shiver. "It was a mutual decision."

"Of course, it was," he mumbled.

"Steph–"

"Don't. Seriously, I get it. It just sucks that's all. You're not giving us any time, Oliver. You can't blame me for being unhappy about this."

"I'm not," I replied. "I get it, but–"

The front door to Abby's house opened and my attention drifted her way. She stepped out wearing a sports bra and way-too-tight yoga pants, causing a low sound to escape my throat.

"Did you just growl?" Stephan chortled.

I ignored his mocking, and fixated on Abby jogging away without giving us a sign of acknowledgement. Her clothing, the running… it was so out of character.

I shook my head, both frustrated and lustfully bothered.

"She's still not talking to you, is she?"

I had mentioned to Stephan about me kissing Abby just before I left the homecoming dance to run after her, but I our conversation cut short since I didn't want to lose sight of her.

"We got into it yesterday," I replied without going into the details. Thinking about it hurt, and the last thing I wanted was to recount what went down between Abby and me. I released another shaky breath. "Will you look after her?"

"Well, if she looks like that every day, I fucking will."

"Don't be a dick. I'm not in the mood."

"Oh, I'm sorry *Mr. I'm-not-in-the-mood*, but have you even seen what she looks like this morning?"

"Did you not just hear me growl right now?"

He laughed and I punched him in the shoulder. In silence, we enjoyed the view until we couldn't see her anymore. It was freezing outside: how she wasn't cold was beyond my me. "When did she start jogging anyway?"

I looked back at him with an incredulous stare. "She doesn't jog you idiot, she probably just saw us sitting here and figured she'd dress up like that to get our attention. I'm sure she's doing it just to piss me off."

"Is it working?"

"What do you think?"

He snickered. "I think she's learning from the best. Kuddos to Abbygail."

I shook my head and laughed harder than I had in days. Stephan would always find a way to make things better, I was really going to miss him. "So, will you?"

"Oliver, don't worry about Abs. She'll be fine; I'm sure of it. But if it makes you feel any better, Tyler and I will look after her."

"Not Tyler."

"Why not Tyler?"

"Because I don't trust him."

"Fine," he chuckled. "I'll be the one looking after her."

I remembered Tyler's hands all over Abby when they were dancing together. It made me uneasy. "Thank you."

Half an hour after climbing back to my room, I noticed Abby jog back to her house. I watched as she slowed her pace and stopped right in the middle of the street. She let her head fall back to face the sky, and letting the light drizzle fall over her face. From where I stool, I noticed her biting the inside of her cheek. I knew what she was doing, unfortunately, even the biting didn't stop her tears. I could see them from the second floor.

When she lowered her eyes back down, she paused at my bedroom window. I was purposefully standing in her line of sight, waiting for her to notice me. But when she did, she frowned and backed away.

I saw the grief; I felt it when she looked at me, but somehow her eyes didn't show sadness, they showed hate.

This isn't the way I wanted this to go.

She wasn't supposed to hate me.

"Oliver," my mother yelled at the sound of shattering glass. I could only imagine her rushing across the hall to meet me in my room. "Oliver what the hell–"

She took my hand. Blood dripped along my arm all the way to the floor, and all I did was look at it. I felt the tears of pain pooling out of my eyes, but they weren't from the stinging shards of glass that pierced through my skin, they were from my heart breaking at the loss of my best friend.

"Sweetheart, what have you done?"

Nothing. That's what I did.

Absolutely nothing.

ABBYGAIL

I wasn't much of a jogger, in fact I hated it just as much as playing any sport that included a ball, but everything in my house reminded me of Oliver, so I dragged my ass outside and started running.

Every step I took away from him felt raw, but with every inhale I realized that being breathless and in physical pain was much better than gasping in tears because of my heart-ache.

Unfortunately, my will to carry on ceased when I turned the corner and saw the skate park. The realization that I would never sit in the bleachers to watch Oliver skateboard, or hide away from our parents to drink a root beer slushy with him, hit me with an even bigger force than I could have anticipated. The fact that we would never sneak out together and cross the gates of the park hand in hand in the middle of the night just to talk, made my lungs constrict tighter, and had me falling to my knees.

With him gone, nothing would ever be the same.

I hadn't heard Stephan's voice when he stopped running a few feet ahead of me. I didn't expect him to walk over to me or hug me without saying a single word.

"Thank you," I whispered, wiping my tears away.

"Anytime, babe."

"Babe?" I raised my eyebrow, sniffling.

"You look like a beach-babe dressed like that." He shrugged. "I'm taking the initiative of giving you a new name. Take it as a compliment."

I smiled and he took off at his regular jogging pace. "See you at school Abs."

The relief didn't last as long as I wished it would have. The closer I got to home, the worse I felt, but it was the sight of him watching me through his bedroom window that made the hurt come back.

Wave. Just wave, Oliver, and it will make everything just a little better...

He didn't wave.

. . .

The lukewarm water soothed my over exhausted muscles, but did nothing for the pain inside soul. Taking a seat in the bathtub, I shut off the cold water completely, and let my sorrows drown under the burning stream.

I welcomed the pain.

Lost in my memories I followed the droplets of water as they tumbled down the grey shower tiles until they reached the tub and made it impossible to separate my tears from bath water as they poured down the drain.

"Abbygail?" My mother banged at the door. "Abby, open up, you've been in there forever."

I knew my mom, if I didn't go to the door, she'd burst in without my permission.

The whole bathroom was filled with steam when I stopped the water and wrapped my body in a towel. My skin itched at the contact of the rough fabric, and as the cloud of misty heat dissipated, I noticed my reddened skin and winced.

"Abby?" My mother gasped as I opened the door. "Honey, what did you do?"

"I'm fine." I replied, recoiling under her touch. "Leave me alone."

"Sweetheart, how hot was that water?"

"Who cares?"

"I care. Abby, this is crazy. You can't do this…your entire body, your skin, it's burnt."

"My skin? This is nothing to what I'm feeling on the inside." I cried. "You don't get it. It hurts. Everything hurts."

"Then let me help you, sweetheart."

I gave my mother a hard stare. "Can you prevent Oliver from leaving?"

She didn't need to answer, her eyes avoiding mine gave me everything I needed to know.

"Then there's nothing you can do." I sneered and walked to my bedroom. "Leave. Me. Alone."

"I left some food on your desk. I want you to eat something. Please—" I slammed the door.

"Jenna?" Oliver's mom knocked and opened our front door as she usually did when she came to our house. I was relieved to hear her walk in. She was preventing me from another awkward talk with my annoying mother. I cracked my bedroom door open and leaned on the frame, listening in on their conversation.

"Evelynn?"

"Hey Jen, I was wondering if you have any extra bandages lying around."

"Of course, I do. What's wrong?"

"Oliver punched his fist through his bedroom window."

"Is he okay?" I could hear the worry in my mother's voice.

"Yeah, I just don't get it. He looked fine when Stephan left, but half an hour later he just lost it and smashed the window. As if I had time for this right now."

"I know what you mean. Abby just got out of the shower, her body looks like she spent an entire day in a suntan machine."

"Are you shitting me? What the hell is going on between those two?"

"I don't know, but you were right. We should have told Abby about Oliver's leaving a few weeks ago. It would have given her time to adjust."

"And probably some time for them to talk about it. I'm really sorry, Jenna."

"Don't be. Seriously, Evy. They've known each other their entire lives; they should be able to figure this out on their own. I promise it will get better."

There was uncertainty in the sound of my mother's voice, but I shut the door to my room and left them to their conversation.

My mother definitely shouldn't be making promises she won't be able to keep...

CHAPTER EIGHTEEN

ABBYGAIL

I was sitting on my bed listening to music when I heard my mother's incessant knocking. She walked in without an invitation and sat down next to me. Her invasions into my personal space were becoming annoying.

"Abby, I've been banging on your door for the past five minutes now."

As if the reason that I couldn't hear what was going on in the outside world wasn't apparent enough, I rolled my eyes and took off my headphones.

"I thought I told you to eat something."

I hadn't eaten a real meal in two days. Why she thought making me a sandwich would be different from anything else she had offered over the few days, I couldn't understand. Simply looking at it made me want to puke. I *had* to throw it out.

"And I thought I told you: I'm. Not. Hungry," I bit back. "I also recall telling you to leave me alone."

Disapproving of my tone, her lips threaded into a thin line. "Oliver's uncle just got here. Come down and say goodbye."

I walked over to the window and watched him talking with his mother by Jerry's truck.

So that's it. He's really leaving...

"Abby?"

"No."

"Abbygail, please. You're going to regret this if you don't come."

The only thing I regret is trusting Oliver.

"I said no." I walked over to my bedroom door and held it opened for her. "He'll be waiting for you, you should go."

Oliver was standing in the light rain, waiting for my mom with open arms when she was crossing the street. I always loved how he and my mother would get along, how she would always smile at his teasing her, or how he could always get us out of trouble with one of his stupid jokes.

After exchanging hugs his eyes sliced to mine standing in my window. The longing sadness we shared was indescribable. We stared at each other for what seemed like an eternity and whatever was going on between us made me realize that I couldn't do it. I couldn't go through his leaving without at least saying goodbye. I took my iPod out.

BlackOrchid: Oliver, I'm sorry. I didn't mean it. I don't hate you. The thing is, everything is so fucked up right now... I don't know how it happened, but I fell in love with you and I've been acting really stupid about it and I'm so, so sorry. It's okay if you don't feel the same, I swear. I don't care about that. What I care about is US. You're my best friend and I can't stand not having you in my life. Just... Please forgive me okay?

I went back to the window waiting to see his face as he read my message. But when I made it to the window he was climbing inside his uncle's truck. I received and instant message the second he slammed the passenger door.

I looked down.

My heart stopped.

Account manager: Undeliverable Message: Olisk8 account is no longer active.

I looked up from the screen and Jerry's truck was

driving away with my best friend in it. It was too late. I was too late. He was gone and neither one of us said goodbye.

The hardest part to watching Oliver disappear in the mist was realizing that I was right all along. Love... one way or another, it always made us lose the most important person in our life.

Love destroyed everything.

OLIVER

I watched her though the passenger seat window as my uncle drove away, and swallowed my tears down as far as I could.

You were supposed to be my best friend, Abbygail. Best friends don't relinquish so easily. They don't yield to a simple obstacle. They fight. They fight for one another, they fight together. You surrendered...

How could you?

CHAPTER NINETEEN

OLIVER

I woke up startled by the flight attendant's rattling concession cart distributing the regular snacks and drinks. As she passed by our seats, I declined her offer. My uncle, on the other hand, ordered himself a bottle of water and dropped a can of soda on my lap. My eyes lowered, bothered by the coldness. I chuckled sarcastically. Of all the drinks he could have picked, he grabbed me a root beer. It was as if life was enjoying my current misery, high fiving itself with every blow it could possibly inflict on my open wounds.

"I already said I didn't want anything."

"Take it, son. You need the energy."

"I am not your son," I replied in anger.

"You're right. I'm sorry."

I shook my head, annoyed. "Just leave me alone, Uncle Jerry."

I stared at my uncle's reflection though the window while pretending to look outside. Aside from being younger by three years, he and my dad looked so much alike, they could have been twins. They had the same dark eyes and tall build, the same crinkle on their forehead when they smiled. The difference was in the way they appeared to people. My uncle was such a serious man compared to my father, that most of the time he looked unapproachable. And ever since his brother passed away, it was ten times worse.

He had a grim smile, probably disappointed by my lack of desire to communicate with him. I didn't care. Bonding with my dad's brother was the last thing I needed.

I wanted my dad.

Period.

No one could replace him.

This is the stupidest idea ever...

Rage pulsed through my veins. I loathed my dad for leaving us, abandoning his battle and conceding to the pain of his wounds, I was mad at my mom for agreeing to leave Carrington, but most of all, my hatred was directed at Abby.

I lifted my legs on my seat and grabbed my knees, shielding my sheepish face from prying eyes. I felt the look of pity in my uncle's silence, but ignored him.

Everything hurt, and all I wanted was to bleed out the incessant agony I carried in my heart.

How could she just give up on us so easily?

"Was that Abby I saw in the window across the street from your house?" my uncle asked, breaking our whole ten minutes of peaceful silence.

"Yup." I kept my eyes closed and faced the wall, hoping he would understand that talking about Abby wasn't a good idea.

"I saw her with you at the funeral. She's gotten hot over the years."

My eyes shot wide open, almost bulging out of my head.

Is he fucking serious? That comment was wrong on so many levels.

I turned my head towards him. "You're kidding, right?"

"Well, no. She's a very pretty girl, Oliver."

"SHE is *sixteen*, Uncle Jerry."

He rolled his eyes at me. "Seriously, Oliver? Do you actually think so little of me?"

I raised my shoulders. There was so much chaos is my head, I wasn't sure about how I felt about anything or anyone, anymore.

"A bit protective, aren't we?" he teased. "I meant that she's turning into a stunning young lady, kid. Guys at school must be lining up to date her."

I muffled a laugh.

If I have my way, Abby won't be dating anyone until she makes it to University.

"I'm actually surprised *you two* aren't an item yet, or haven't been at least. I don't think I've ever seen two friends being so drawn to one another, before."

"Yeah, so I've been told," I muttered.

He looked at me inquisitively. "Your mom tells me you and Abbygail got into a pretty big fight before you left. Do you want to talk about it?"

I put my headphones over my ears and turned my music on, making it clear we were done with our conversation.

"Is that why she didn't come down to say goodbye? She looked pretty sad in that window of hers."

I took off my headphones. "What part of my putting these over my head don't you understand, Uncle Jerry? I don't want to talk about it. Not with you. Not with anyone. Abbygail, is off *any* conversation limits. Got it?"

He took my iPod away from my hands. "She's your best friend, Oliver."

"You know nothing about us," I sneered. "Nothing. But let me clue you in since you seem so interested in my life for the first time in... ever. She and I are over. Whatever we had got destroyed the moment I admitted to her that I was moving to B.C." I could feel the screeching pain making its way up to my throat. I was ready to explode. "Now can we just please not talk about this anymore?"

"Time has a way of healing things," he replied confidently.

"Time will heal nothing. Just goes to show how little you know of Abby and me. She will *never* forgive me for leaving her."

"Oliver, I know you're second guessing yourself right now. Changing homes, schools, friends, after all you've already been through; it's rough. But I want to remind you that you chose this and you did for a reason. Try to remember them."

Trust me, I'm trying...

I'm trying pretty fucking hard right now.

"You don't get it, Uncle Jerry, I don't want time. I want *her*. I miss her. This moving away thing, it's the stupidest idea I ever had. I can't do this."

Finally understanding that it was his silence that I was desperately craving, he handed me my iPod back.

"You know what, kid? I'm going to give you the best advice your father ever gave me many years ago. I live with his words of wisdom every day, and it's exactly what he would tell you if he was here with us." I eyed him curiously. He had my full attention. "Don't live with regrets, Oliver. Nothing good ever comes out of them."

CHAPTER TWENTY

ABBYGAIL

My off-again-on-again relationship with Oliver should have been a good training method for his leaving, but seriously, nothing compared to his true absence. I couldn't feel him anymore, and every time I came to the realization that he wasn't within reach, I felt the incessant growing pain in the depth of my heart. It was weird to watch the whole world continue to revolve even though my own felt like it had stopped.

The constant ache and emptiness I felt kept me unfocused all day and up all night.

All I wanted was for it to stop.

As the hours drew into days, and days ticked into weeks, I felt numb. I did nothing except what I was told. I got up in the morning, got dressed, went to school, came home, did my homework, my chores, and went to bed. I tried to eat, but more often than not my food ended up in the garbage. My body was wasting away. My mom was worried about me, and so were my friends. Whenever they tried to help or intervene, I got angry. The only thing that seemed to work and calm me down was the sound of the rustling branches that came from my willow tree. Something about them helped sooth my pain, but it was never for very long. As soon as the wind died down, so did the quietness in my heart.

"Abbygail?" Stephan called, stepping out from my backyard patio door. "I just spoke with your mom, she said you were out here. Do you mind if I join you?"

I shrugged indifferently. I knew very well that he never would have shown up here alone if Oliver was around. He walked down the wooden stairs to join me.

"Can I sit?"

I was lying on the comforter Oliver and I always used when we spent our late nights out, and moved over. Stephan was bulkier than Oliver. It's what made him a good running-back. If I wasn't accustomed to him, I would have been scared to turn on his bad side, but to me, he was just like a big teddy bear.

"How are you holding up?" he asked. He took a seat and leaned on the trunk beside me.

"I'm good, you?"

"Likewise, I guess. Do you miss him?"

I snorted.

What a stupid question.

"Why are you here, Stephan?" I asked. I was suddenly very annoyed by his unexplained presence.

"I came to see how you were doing. You didn't show up at Liam's party like you said you would. We're all pretty worried about you, Abby."

"Well, don't be. I'll be fine." I hid my head between my knees and put my hand over it so he wouldn't see me crying again.

"Abbygail–"

"Let's say you're playing a football game," I interrupted, facing him. Who cared about my tears anyway? "And you're about to receive the ball from your quarterback, but the offensive player takes you by surprise and slams right into you head first, hitting you right in the gut the exact moment you're finally able to catch the ball. How would you feel?"

"Fucking pissed?" he replied, amused by my question.

Such a typical guy answer...

"No, I mean physically. How does it feel?"

"Well I guess if I'm not expecting the hit, then I can't protect myself. Can I?"

I shook my head, not that it made much difference with the end result.

"I'd say that I would probably be out of breath for a

few seconds."

I looked into his eyes so that he could grasp onto what I was trying to make him understand. "That's how I'm doing, Stephan. Except, it's not that I can't breathe for a few seconds, it's like I can't breathe all the fucking time." Tears were running down my face, again. "Everyone wants me to move on, or tells me that Oliver's leaving isn't the end of the world. It is to me. No one gets it. Oliver and I have spent almost every waking moment of our lives together. Hell, I'm unable to count the nights we haven't spent together in the past year, and now, he's gone.

"I mean, I get it. I understand why he left. I'm not selfish. I never would have held him back, especially if it's to help himself get better. I don't want him taking drugs, or have him spiraling out of control. I want him happy and healthy, but he gave me less than forty-eight hours to get used to this and he left without saying goodbye. Am I not allowed to deal with this in my own way? His leaving hurts."

"Come here." He lifted me effortlessly and settled me on his lap. Without saying a word, he let me cry on his shoulder.

The branches of the willow tree rustled with the cold breeze. I pulled Stephan's arms tighter around me and I listened to the soothing sound of his heartbeat mixed with the whispering of the remaining leaves.

"Are you asleep?" Stephan asked, breaking the

silence.

I had stopped crying and we were just sitting quietly, listening to the wind. "No"

But I haven't felt this calm in weeks

"I do have a favor to ask though."

"I'm all ears, Babe."

I let out a soft chuckle. I still couldn't wrap my head around the nickname he decided to give me. "Um... well, I know this is going to sound weird, and please don't read anything into it because I swear it's nothing more than what I'm asking."

"Okay?"

"Would you mind spending the night with me?"

He pulled my shoulders away from his chest to look at me and raised his eyebrow. "Are you sure this isn't you asking me to sleep with you? 'Cause I'm not sure I'm quite comfortable with this new admission of yours, Abbygail."

I smirked and playfully smacked him on the shoulder. "I just told you to not read into it you perv."

"And there's that smile that I love." He chuckled. "I was kidding. And yes, Abs, I'm in."

Stephan looked at me curiously when I held out Oliver's old football jersey for him to sleep in. It was obvious that he was wondering why I still had his clothing in my drawer, he just didn't look comfortable asking. Oliver hadn't claimed the stuff he left in my room before he left and the truth was, even if he had, I wouldn't have given them back.

"I have a bunch of them," I specified in response to his non-verbal question. "He left his stuff lying around like my room was his own personal space all the time."

"Really? Didn't bother you?"

I shook my head. "No. I did the same at his place."

Except my stuff is now neatly put away in my own drawers and closet.

Stephan shook his head. "I've said it before and I'll say it again: you two are the weirdest best friends on the planet."

I grabbed my own shirt and boxers and stepped out in the hallway with a tight smile.

Were. We were the weirdest best friends...

I watched Stephan wandering around my room when I came back from the bathroom. His attention was fixated on my walls. They were covered in pictures of Oliver and me. I studied him stopping ever so often and grinning at some of the pictures. "That's when I turned four."

He startled at my interruption.

"My father took the picture of Oliver and me at the Orchard in Westminster."

The curiosity in his eyes didn't go unnoticed. "I don't think I've ever heard you talk about your dad before."

I raised my shoulders. It was true. I rarely spoke of him with my other friends. I had in the past, when I was much younger, but at the age of sixteen, I compared my relationship with Simon to an old piece of pizza in a greasy cardboard box: unappealing and unwanted.

"There's not much to say. He left us the same year we took the picture. End of story."

"I'm really sorry, Abs"

"About who? Simon? Trust me, Steph, you have nothing to be sorry about."

He didn't seem convinced by my answer, but didn't push the subject further. "Well I didn't mean to pry. It's just that it's a nice picture of you two, that's all."

"Stephan," I assured. "I'm not the kind of person who cares about people looking at my stuff. Trust me. You wouldn't be here if I was. As for my father? He left. I don't talk about him because I don't care for him."

I walked over to my nightstand, dropped my clothing in the hamper, and took a frame off the wall, handing it to Stephan.

"Hey, was this on the first of July?"

I nodded smiling. It was a picture of Oliver and him sitting on my backyard deck, talking to each other with the sun setting to their right side. It was a perfect image of their chemistry.

"This picture is awesome, Abs. Who took it?"

"I'm guessing Tyler did with Henry's camera. You know how much he likes taking pictures. Oliver has the same one in his room."

Had, not has. Fuck this is going to take a lot of getting used to...

Stephan didn't notice my mishap, but said nothing. He simply admired the picture silently for a while. I could tell he missed his best friend just as much as I did.

"Keep it," I offered when he tried to hang the frame back on my wall. "It's yours."

"Thanks, Abby, but I can't take it."

"I want you to have it, Stephan. He was your best friend, and you deserve it even more than I do. Besides..." I tried to smile. "My room is covered in pictures of him. One less won't make a difference."

"But then you won't have one of me," he teased.

"I will." I grinned. "Soon enough."

By the way Stephan was laying on my bed, breathing quietly, I knew that he couldn't be as comfortable as he was claiming to be. The silence between us felt awkward.

"What are you thinking about?" I asked breaking the stillness.

"Honestly?" he replied, turning to face me. "About how pissed Oliver would be if he found out that you and I were sharing the same bed right now. I doubt his asking me to look after you meant he was okay with the idea of me sharing a bed with you."

My brows furrowed. "Oliver asked you to look after me?" I wasn't sure I wanted Stephan in my room anymore. "I don't need a babysitter Stephan."

"You're right, you don't. You need a friend. I'm that friend. And I would have done it anyway, Abby. My being here has nothing to do with him. We're friends. Looking after each other is what we're supposed to do."

"Do you really believe he'd mind that you're spending the night with me?"

"Mind? Fuck that, Babe. He'd be furious, and if he knew we were under the same bed covers right now, he'd fly all the way back and beat the shit out of me. But honestly, I don't care. You smiled tonight, Abs. I haven't seen your smile since I called you Babe in the skate park. So I could care less how Oliver feels about us spending tonight or any other night for that matter, together."

Stephan stretched his arm around me and pulled me closer to him.

"I miss him so much, Steph."

"I know, Babe, I do too. Have you thought about writing to him? Maybe it could help."

"I tried. He unsubscribed his messenger account."

"Yeah, he told me he would. I think Oliver wanted

to detach himself from us. Makes saying goodbye easier. You know?"

I shook my head. "No. I don't. It's stupid. Cutting himself off like we don't matter is ridiculous."

"He didn't do it because we don't matter, Abby. He did it because we matter too much. Just write him a letter the old-fashioned way, through the postal service. I'm pretty sure your mother has their new address."

I yawned, hugging my pillow tighter. "I'll think about it."

"What did you write when you found out his account was closed?" Stephan asked after a few minutes of silence.

"I told him why I was acting stupid, that I was sorry about everything that was going on, and that I hadn't meant it when I said that I hated him."

"I'm pretty sure he knows that already."

"Maybe." I shrugged. "I wish we–I regret not saying goodbye."

He shut my night lamp off and put his hand over my stomach. "It isn't goodbye, Abbygail. It's a 'see you later.'"

Silent tears ran down my face again. "I'm in love with my best friend, Stephan."

"I know." He tightened his hold on me. "It will get easier, Abs. I promise."

CHAPTER TWENTY-ONE

OLIVER

B.C. was beautiful. The trees, the mountains... it was a sight I would never get tired of. The house Uncle Jerry had found for my mother and me was great. It was large and only one-story high compared to our cottage house in Carrington, but it was perfect for the both of us. Its big windows and fancy woodwork build sat on the cliff side of our neighborhood. The view was extraordinary, especially on clear nights where I could see the many stars illuminating the dark sky and snowy mountain tops.

My first week in school was a challenge. Vancouver was a big town and Clover High was a big school, but at least I wasn't the guy that lost his father anymore. I was the new kid that everyone was curious about. And luckily enough, I managed to make a couple of friends within the first few weeks. The only downside to my arriving so late in the school year was that I wasn't sure I would make the football team for the remainder of the season. I'd have to rely on Kayden, the coach's son, to convince his father that I could stick around to show off my skills.

"Oh, hey you're home." my mom said as I opened the front door. She was taking out the trash.

I took the bags out of her hands and dumped them in the can at the end of the driveway for her. "How was your day?"

"Thank you. It was okay, how was school?"

"It was cool. I met with Kayden's dad on the field today. The guys and I were passing the football at lunch time. Coach said he'd like for me to attend practice next week."

She seemed pleased by the news. The fact that I had reconsidered playing made her smile every time I talked about it. "Here, you got this in the mail this morning."

I took the envelope out of her hand and smiled. I'd recognized her perfect handwriting among hundreds.

"I haven't seen that face in a while," my mother remarked. "Who's the letter from?"

I looked up to see her soft eyes watching me. "It's from Abby."

Hey Oliver,

So... right, this is weird. Um... how are you? How's your new house, your new school? Have you made any friends? Did you make the football team? I really hope you did, and if you didn't because you're too late for the season, trust me, they're missing out. The Giants lost their last game, just so you know. They're missing a huge piece without you being here. I keep hearing how much the guys miss you. The cheerleaders miss you too. There, that should make you feel a bit better. Ha.

But no one misses you like I do...

Okay, so here's the thing. I'M SORRY. I didn't mean any of what I said. Well technically that's not true. I meant most of what I said the last time we talked. I do need you, and I do love you, and I really hate that you left. But I don't hate you.

I could never hate you.

Oliver, you mean the world to me, and it hurts me that you left, but what hurts me more is that you felt that you couldn't tell me that you were leaving. We never keep stuff from each other, Oliver, and we never lie to each other either. That's how we work. It's how we've always worked.

So, here's me being 100% honest. Not having you here, it's tough. Some days I think that dying would be easier. I look like shit, I feel like shit, and I'm tired of crying all the time. So, as you can see, I'm not

taking the whole thing very well. But I'll try ok?
Because in the end what counts is that you're doing
better.
Stephan helps. He slept over the other night. He's the
one who suggested I should try writing you a letter.
I'm not even sure if I'm going to send it or not...
I tried texting you before you climbed in the truck. I
really would have liked you reading my message; it
explained a whole lot of things...
Anyway, I guess all that I wanted to say is that I'm
sorry. I wish things could have been different for us,
but I guess our destinies decided otherwise.
I miss you Oliver. I dream about you every night...
it's the only solace I get.
Love,
Abbygail xxx

I must have been grinning like an idiot, well, part
of me was anyway. The thought of Stephan sharing a
bed with my girl didn't sit with me very well.

He and I are definitely going to talk about this...

There was no way I could count the number of
times Abby had apologized first in one of our
arguments. Even when she was wrong, she always
found a way to turn it around for it to be my fault. But
as I read her letter, I couldn't help believing that it was
my turn to take responsibility. It really was my fault
that things went down the way they did. Abbygail

might not have known every detail of my reasons for leaving, but her letter showed that she understood part of why I had to go. Her not being angry with me, helped me be at peace with the choices I had made for the both of us. Nevertheless, she and I needed to talk, we both knew that, but every time I picked up the phone to dial her number, fear stopped me. No words could make up for what happened between us.

My beautiful best friend haunted my every dream since my leaving home, yet I found my comfort and happiness in them. But the nights where I woke up short of breath, sweating and searching for my best friend's hand were tough. I knew that leaving her behind would be hard on us, but anticipation is never as harsh as the reality. Abby was right: being close for so long made us being apart very hard to adapt to.

Drawing out my pen, I replied at the end of her letter. With every word I made sure she knew how much she was missed and how sorry I was. But mostly she needed to know that even though we were apart, our relationship would never be over. Sliding the letter back inside her envelope, I laughed at my own joke, wrote 'return to sender' over my address and mailed our letter back home.

CHAPTER TWENTY-TWO

OLIVER

So, your house is sold. But I guess you knew that already. My mom said all the paper stuff was done by mail and fax machines, which means it's been going on behind my back for at least a week.
I'm not going to lie, this really sucks, Oliver. It makes everything real, you know? I guess its official now, you really aren't coming back...
Oh, right, shoot!
Hi Oliver, how are you?
Okay, pleasantries over.
So I know I told you that I was accepting your moving away... Wait. Did I say that? Because I don't think I did, and if I did, I just want to make sure

that you understand that accepting does not mean that I agree with it, nor does it mean that I don't want you back, because I do. Like a lot!

Anyway, it doesn't matter. I promise I'm doing better, but this whole thing, new neighbors and stuff, it's not going to work with me. I'm going to pretend to be fine with it but I mean... really?

You could have called to tell me, you know. Noticing the sold sign when I came back from school was NOT COOL, Oliver Langton!

Ah crap, I have to go. Someone's at the door and Mom's not home.

Hey Oliver,

Sorry about yesterday... I met the new owners and then my mom took me out for dinner. Anyway, the new family moving into your old house doesn't look as bad as I had thought they would. They seem traditional enough. You know, mom and dad with two kids. Sophia, the girl, she's like the same age as Cole... you know, my next-door neighbor that insists he'll marry me one day? Hopefully his crush will move on to her soon enough. LOL

Wait. Did I just? See what your leaving is doing to me? I'm using stupid abbreviations now... please, Oliver, come back... come back and save me from myself!

Ugh, just shoot me already. Okay, I'm done ranting now.

So anyway, the guy's name is Chase, he looks older than us though. Like eighteen maybe? I don't know... anyway it doesn't matter. What matters is that their parents asked me if I would be interested in babysitting Sophia twice a week because Chase has some sports thing after school. Since I have no reason to go to football practice anymore, I said yes. Between babysitting her, and Cole, I'll be loaded by X-mas time. Okay, so it's getting late and I have to study. Mr. Fontaine stuck us with a math exam tomorrow morning, and I really need to pass this one otherwise I'll need to stay after for catching up classes. You know as much as I do that detention with Mrs. Beaudoin is much more fun than an extra hour with Mr. Fontaine, especially since you're not here to play hangman with me. I'll write to you tomorrow okay? Love you.

Hey Oliver,

Okay, so I'm going to allow myself to say this once in my life, because it sure as hell better NEVER happen again...

Having a night out for your birthday without your best friend, is unnatural. Just wait 'til yours comes up. And now that I think about it, why haven't you called? You'd better have a damn good excuse or else you will owe me a whole lot of root beer slushies when I see you.

Have you ever noticed that when we hang out as a group we always split into pairs? You know Ava and Kylie, Stephan and Tyler, Zoey and whatever extra guy is invited to join in that particular day, and then there's you and me. I had never paid attention to this minor detail before today. Guess who got stuck spending a whole lot of time by herself today? That's right: Me.

Yes, I know... on my own birthday!

Can you believe them? I swear I'm not saying this because I want you to feel bad, it's just... I miss us Oliver. Nobody enjoys my stupid jokes or foolishness like you do. Everything is changing. I don't like being apart from you. I miss you. I miss spending time with you.

I really hope I'll be hearing from you soon.

Abby

xxx

"Oliver?" my mother shouted, slamming the front door behind her. "I need your help with these."

I crossed the hall from my room and saw her in the entrance. Her hands were full of grocery bags, and she was completely soaked from the rain.

"You sold the house?" I scowled.

Her face fell along with the bags she was holding onto. "Who told you?"

"What does it matter who? How can you not tell me stuff like this?

"It was Abby, wasn't it?"

"MOM. I learned this over a stupid letter." I shook the envelope angrily at my mother's face. "Tell me, why did I have to learn this in her letter?"

"Oliver I'm–"

"You know what? It doesn't matter. I'm out. Don't wait up for dinner." I stormed pass her without giving her a second glance.

I walked in the rain for a while, anger and sadness was eating me up from inside. I hated that my mother had sold my childhood home. Knowing that it was still ours reassured me in some way that we still had somewhere to go if, or when, I'd be ready to go back. Now we had nothing that linked us to our family anymore. And something inside me told me that I was going to lose it all sooner rather than later.

As I made my way down the hill, I spotted the empty skate park. It was always unoccupied. Maybe it was the wet weather that kept the kids away… who knew? But one thing was for sure I was pretty pissed off at myself for somehow losing my board in our moving.

After finding a dry spot under a ramp, I took

Abby's letter out and read it a second time. I missed her. Her letters helped, but not being able to see her and touch her was getting really hard. My mother and I had gone shopping for her birthday over the weekend. I took out her gift from my pocket, and twirled around the fragile white gold charm bracelet. On it, I added all the things that reminded me of her: a black bow because she always had one in her hair, an orchid because it was her favorite flower, a blue teardrop because it reminded me of her eyes, and a heart because I needed her to remember that I loved her regardless of what was going on between us. I also added a skateboard, hoping that every time she wore it she'd be reminded of me.

I drew out my pen and replied to her the same way I had in her first letter. When I was done I slipped the white gold charm bracelet inside, mailed the envelope and walked back home.

Over the weeks after arriving in Vancouver, my mother and I had been learning how to live our lives without my dad, which also meant getting to know each other all over again. But in all honesty, I was keeping a lot from her. Most of it was my ambivalent feelings towards moving. I couldn't say that I was regretting my decision to leave Carrington because everything was going so well in B.C., but I would be lying if I said that I didn't miss our home.

I felt many things when I walked back to our new house: resentment, anger, longing, sadness… but it was the weight I was carrying on my shoulders that was tremendous. My mother had made many sacrifices by moving, and I had yet to thank her and apologize for my involvement in my father's death. When I walked in on my mother crying at the dining room table, I felt the remorse hit me with a force I hadn't expected. Blowing up in my mother's face for something that was bound to happen sooner or later wasn't very considerate of me. And I knew my mom, selling our home was hurting her just as much as it was hurting me.

"Mom?" I hesitated, stepping into the dining room.

Her sad eyes shifted to mine. Pain radiated in her silence. I took a seat by her side and after hugging her tightly, she and I had the talk we should have had months ago.

CHAPTER TWENTY-THREE

OLIVER

My mother and I had planned to surprise Aunt Jenna for her birthday on the last weekend of November. I was really looking forward to going back to Carrington, we had our entire trip planned out, but then the day before we intended to leave for our vacation, I came home from school to my disappointed mother. It turned out there was an emergency at work, and she needed to be there and work on both days.

The only high point of that week was when my she had surprised me with a cute baby American bulldog that same weekend. She had a white coat with little black spots everywhere and I adored her feisty attitude. She was exactly like my Abby, which is probably why I named her Freckles.

Freckles and I had been out for at least fifteen minutes playing fetch before I needed to catch the bus to school. When the post office truck rolled up the street, she dropped the ball and I was officially off pitcher duty. Her protective radar had officially switched on, and nothing was to take her away from her guarding responsibilities.

I couldn't help but laugh at her behavior when someone approached her territory. She had been living at our house for a total of six days, yet every time someone came close to it, Freckles went full-on into her defensive mode. She made it her daily objective to scare our visitors away with her cute little barks.

When our mailman stepped out of his truck to deliver our mail, Freckles took a seat at my feet and let out a warning growl.

"Do you think she'll get used to me coming here every couple of days?" he asked, kneeling at her feet.

She let out a cautionary snarl when he got too close to us.

Yeah, pup, your name fits you perfectly!

"For your sake," I chuckled, "I hope she does!"

I recognized Abby's handwriting the second he handed me our mail. "Have a nice day, kid. You too Freckles."

Hey Oliver,

You'll never believe me, but Kylie and Stephan are dating. I knew Stephan liked her. He's been raving about her every time we go out for a run. It was getting annoying. Yeah, you read it right, I run with Stephan now. We do it at least three times a week. My stamina isn't as good as his, but I am getting pretty good.

Anyway, I'm totally getting off topic. So, I also knew that Kylie liked Stephan, but you know how she is with her school and stuff, always setting her boring priorities first... Well, Tuesday night we went to the movies, he asked her out and she said yes. He is absolutely adorable with her. I swear I never saw Stephan like that with a girl. He's completely whipped and it is hilarious!

And speaking of dating, there is something I've been meaning to say for a while now... you and I are currently in a sort of predicament Mr. Langton. For some reason I don't quite understand, the guys in school are under the impression that they are not allowed to date me. Would you care to explain?

Because after asking around a little, it turns out that you have some rule about dating me that I didn't know about? And apparently, it's been going on for quite a while now... If you aren't sure what I'm talking about, let me refresh your memory. They call

*it the: Don't touch Abbygail Evens or Oliver
Langton will kill you rule.*

First off, what the hell is this rule about?

*And secondly, I mean seriously? You'd think that
these guys would be smart enough to realize that you
living across the country, kind of voids the non-
dating rule.*

As if you'd come back just to kick their ass...

Wait.

Holly crap I just had an epiphany.

*Scratch that, I just had two epiphanies... and just to
clue you in, remember Mason? Yeah, that guy. I'm
calling him after I'm done with your letter.*

*So just in case you haven't noticed, I have an issue
with your rule, Oliver. I'm in high school. I'm
allowed to date. So you'd better find a way to fix our
problem, soon, otherwise I'm going to ruin your
brand-new skateboard with pink and purple flowers,
and so much glitter that every time you want to use
it, you'll need to put plastic bags over your shoes.
Capisce?*

*And what about you? I mean, I bet a bunch of girls
fell for the new guy, and can't wait to get their hands
on you. You don't see me sending them threatening
letters to not touch my best friend. Fix this, Oliver!
Hey, I thought for sure you guys would have come
down last weekend since it was my mother's
birthday and all, but I guess your mom might not*

want to travel right now. I get it though. Anyway, since you guys didn't come, my mom and I went on a shopping trip in Toronto for her birthday. I got a bunch of new stuff. You should see my new Rolling Stone t-shirt. Yes, I know, I already have one. But that one's old and it's all worn out, I <u>needed</u> another one, you could totally see my bra through the old tank top. I don't get why you never told me this before, by the way.

Oh, and I got you your X-Mas gift too. It's not quite ready yet but you'll see it's awesome.

See Oliver, we can be friends. I can do this, I'm getting better at it, I promise. Please write back to me, I miss you and you're so important to me. Don't give up on our friendship okay?

Abby

xxx

It was when I read her last lines that it finally dawned on me that Abby wasn't reading my replies.

If she isn't reading them, then where the hell are they going?

CHAPTER TWENTY-FOUR

ABBYGAIL

"Abby?" my mother called from the entrance door. "Are you sure you're not feeling well enough to come with me? It's just breakfast, and if you don't want to eat, it's fine with me."

I shook my head even though she couldn't see me, and walked out of my room to see her out. "I'm sorry, Mom. I know you really wanted me to come and meet your friend, but I'm honestly not feeling all that hot."

"You don't look that bad to me. When's the last time you said you threw up? It's pretty weird that I haven't heard you."

I shrugged. "Considering your room is on the opposite side of the house, it's not weird at all. And I don't know what time it was, checking the clock wasn't really one of my priorities, Mom"

I could tell she was disappointed that I would be staying home alone on Christmas morning. Faking an illness was the only way I knew she would agree without her fighting me. She really wanted me to join her and her friends; it was the third time she had asked me since we woke up. I didn't want to go. I found the idea of slouching on my couch way more appealing than having a Christmas brunch at Rington's Bed and Breakfast.

"I know you're worried about me, but I promise I'll be fine at home. I'm actually kind of feeling a little bit better already. I just don't think I should risk going and then end up puking my guts at the restaurant. Plus, I wouldn't mind some sleep. My upset stomach kept me awake all night."

"Fine."

"I'm willing to make you a deal, though. If after my nap I feel better and you aren't home yet, I'll bake you some cookies. Did you have any preferences?" I asked as she put her coat on.

She eyed me suspiciously.

Maybe the cookie thing was a bit much...

"I've been craving your Triple Chocolate delights for months. You know the cookies *Oliver* loves. They have the melted chocolate in the middle. You remember, right?" She wasn't doing it on purpose. I knew that. But the sound of Oliver's name inflicted much more pain than anyone could possibly imagine. It bothered me that I was still without news from him, and my pretending to be sick and wanting to stay home was for that exact reason.

If there was one moment where I hoped I would hear anything from him, Christmas was it. It was our holiday; the one we always spent as a family. Unfortunately, he didn't come home, and the last thing I felt like doing was putting on a fake smile, pretending I was okay.

I wasn't okay. Far from it, actually.

And while I understood why they wouldn't make the trip, it didn't make it hurt any less. Hope was a strong feeling, and where Oliver was concerned, mine was dying slowly.

As the weeks had turned into months, I began to wonder if Oliver was just ignoring my attempts to make things right because he was still mad at me or maybe if in his eyes, our friendship really was over.

I grabbed my head and massaged my temples at my last thought.

"Are you sure you're going to be sick again? I can stay home if you'd prefer."

I sighed. "No. I'm fine, Mom. It's just a headache. I'll grab a couple of Tylenols and go lie down as soon as you leave."

"Okay. Call me if you need anything." She blew me

a kiss and stepped out the door.

I exhaled loudly at the sight of the empty loveseat. Watching 'Home Alone' with my best friend was our yearly tradition, and even though it felt wrong to do it without him, it also felt wrong not to do it at all. I grabbed my favorite comforter and my box of Froot-Loops, popped in the DVD, and sat on my friend-less couch.

It was about twenty minutes into the movie when I heard the first set of knocking at my door.

"Go away!" I grumbled to no one but myself. I was finally getting to the moment where Kevin would realize that his family left for their trip without him, and I didn't feel like getting up.

When the sound of the doorbell interrupted the movie a second time, I pressed pause and went to see who my intruder was. I looked out of the side window and saw Sophia standing outside my house looking like a stuffed teddy bear with her oversized pink winter suit.

I opened the door. "Hello?"

"Merry Christmas, Abbygail," she shouted

"Thanks, Sophia. You too." I pretended to smile. "Um, what can I do for you?"

Sophia was a sweet kid, but she made a habit of crossing the street and paying me a visit every time she got bored. At first, I thought it was cute. After a while, it kind of became tiresome.

"I wanted to know if you wanted to come and play outside with me and Chase?"

I looked over Sophia's shoulder and sure enough her brother was standing right behind her watching me with his sexy smirk. When I realized that his eyes were directed at the middle section of my body and not my face, I looked down at my worn-out sweatpants and tank top, and rolled my eyes.

You have got to be kidding me.

I crossed my arms over my chest, and waited to see how long it would take for him to realize that I'd noticed him staring at my chest. It took less than ten seconds, and when he looked up, I cocked my head to the side.

"So, Abby, do you want to come out or not?" Sophia asked, interrupting my staring competition with her brother.

I looked over at my living room couch and then back to my next-door neighbors standing in front of me expectantly.

The hell with it, Macaulay Culkin isn't going anywhere, he can wait an hour.

"Sure, Sophia, I'll get dressed and join you outside. Go knock on Cole's door, he might want to join us."

She squealed at the idea as if it was the best thing she had ever heard in her entire life, and ran to the other house.

"I'm sorry about the staring."

I shot him an eye roll and reached for my winter boots. "Of course, you are. So, aren't you a missing a couple of pieces of clothing to play in the snow?"

"Do I look like a guy that wants to play outside? My mom kicked us out. Apparently, we have too much energy for her to cook and clean before our guests come over tonight," he complained. "She says she can't focus or whatever. And just before you ask, Sophia's the overly excited one."

"Of course, she is," I mocked, once more.

Chase was the complete opposite of Oliver. He was sweet, but there was a pretentious side to him that people, especially my friends, didn't really like. Since he was a year older than we were, we didn't see him all that much. He had his own group of friends which were mostly his basketball teammates. To be honest, they were pretty rowdy, and Chase wasn't any different. Ever since he'd moved into Oliver's house from his hometown in Kingston, they hadn't lost a game, and their success fueled their pride.

I didn't know Chase all that well. I saw him when he would take over his sister's care, and that was about the extent of our encounters. Once in a while he would ask me to stick around and watch one of Sophia's boring TV shows with them, so I would, but he and I rarely talked. My reasons for staying were mostly because I needed to take my mind off every other crappy aspect of my life.

I would be lying if I said that sitting in Oliver's house didn't feel comforting to me.

Being around Chase made me nervous, though, and somehow, I think he knew. He was obviously cute, with his short sandy blond hair, light hazel eyes and sporty look, but I wasn't attracted to him. Well, I was —kind of—but I definitely wasn't interested in him in that way. My heart belonged to the guy that had moved into a time zone different than mine.

My feelings for Oliver hadn't changed.

I still felt his lips on mine every time I shut my eyes. I still dreamed of him every time I fell asleep. And his football jersey was still my favorite —everything.

I shut the door behind us and noticed the snow covering the ground. Breathing in the cold air, I watched Cole and Sophia run around. I couldn't help feeling the hollowness inside my heart. Both reminded me of Oliver and me, attacking each other with their slushy snowballs.

"Hey, what's up with you? Are you okay?"

I wiped the tear threatening to roll down my cheek. "Yeah. I'm fine. Do you want to join them?"

"No," he laughed. "If I *have* to play outside, I'll be building a snowman. I'm not the cat and mouse kind of person."

I frowned, wondering how he could not get that running around in the snow was one of the best perks of winter. Or maybe that was just an Oliver and Abbygail thing?

"So, what do you say? Are you joining me or not?"

"Sure."

Any distraction is a good distraction.

We were mounting up the head of the snowman when Cole and Sophia decided to finally stop teasing each other and give us a hand. Unfortunately, whatever assistance they were trying to give, ended up being worse than if they hadn't helped at all. Everything kept falling over, so I sent them out back to pick up some sticks and stones for the body parts.

As I bent over trying to fix the middle body, I felt Chase coming from behind. I turned to face him just in time to see the huge lump of snow hovering over my head.

"Don't you dare," I warned.

He flashed me an evil grin. "It's cute how you seem to believe that warning me will actually prevent me from doing this."

I tried to move away but I wasn't quick enough. Chase dropped everything he was holding on top of my head, and roared in laughter at the surprised expression on my face. "Absolutely perfect."

I popped a brow and charged, making him fall to the ground at the impact of our bodies. The fact that he wasn't expecting the hit was hilarious. I laughed so hard I could barely breathe. Unfortunately, my power over him didn't last very long. Within an instant I found myself on my back with him straddling me. He pushed away a lump of wet hair away from my face and I shivered.

"Cold?" he asked without taking his piercing gaze away from mine.

I shook my head and we both remained still. We stared at each other until we heard his mother calling them inside for lunch.

"I really like your smile, Abbygail Evens," Chase whispered into my ear. "You should definitely do it more often."

I was sure he was about to kiss me. Part of me wanted him to so that I'd know how it felt to be kissed by someone who wasn't Oliver, but the other part felt relieved when he got up and called his sister to go back home.

What the hell just happened?

My ass was numb and wet, yet I was unable to will myself to move. Chase turned around as he crossed the street, and smiled at my frozen body.

"Later, Abby."

It took me a second to process a reply. "Why later?"

"Because you and your mom are coming over for dinner."

I frowned. "We are?"

He didn't reply. He simply winked and walked inside his house.

. . .

I was being watched. I felt it in the heavy silence. The wind kicked up, briskly blowing the cold against my wet face. It was raging so hard I could hear the wrestling branches of the willow tree all the way to the front of the house.

Chills ran up my spine.

I tried to shelter the sting by turning my head against the headwind, and that's when I saw him with his back to me. I stood as he started to walk away. Something inside me told me I should be trying to get his attention.

"Oliver?" I whispered.

I squinted my eyes in order to get a better view.

Impossible. I have to be hallucinating. Why would Oliver come all the way here and not come to the house?

I shook my head.

Abs, maybe you really are coming down with something.

I ignored the screaming voice inside my head. I ignored the pain in my gut, and even though every bone in my body was urging me to call after the unknown silhouette, I didn't. I just watched him walk away from me, focusing on the sound of his footsteps as he increased the distance between us.

CHAPTER TWENTY-FIVE

OLIVER

"So let me get this straight," Kayden argued. We were sitting on the couch in my room playing Madden on my PlayStation. "You just stood there watching her and did nothing?"

"What was I supposed to do?"

"I don't know, go up to her and say something?"

"Really? Like what?"

"Well by this point I'd say anything would have worked. But 'hi' and 'how are you', could have been a damn good start. Even a 'why the hell was this guy straddling your body,' would have worked."

My mother hadn't been able to take any time off work for the holidays, but she really wanted to go back home for Christmas, so we went even though it cost her a ridiculous amount of money for just a few days. It was a brief trip. We got there late on the twenty-third, spent the night and the following day with my Aunt Hailey that lived in the town next to Carrington. Then, on Christmas morning, before catching our flight back to BC, my mother had plans for us to have lunch with Jenna.

I was really looking forward to seeing Abby, but then her mother told us Abby had been sick all night and that she wanted to stay home. I don't know if I felt worried or aggravated by her lack of showing up, but I left the bed and breakfast and walked home with every intention of knocking on her door myself.

I was expecting her to be sitting on the couch watching 'Home Alone' all the while hoping that I would show up. What I wasn't expecting was to see her laughing and smiling with people that weren't me.

I watched her as she wrestled with the guy our age that I didn't know. I watched as he sat over her body, so close to her beautiful face and whispered something that made her smile. I would have given anything to see the color of her eyes, needing to know exactly what she was feeling, but I froze because jealousy ate me up from the inside.

I turned around because I hated it. I left because I felt replaced.

"I think he was going to kiss her."

Kayden started to laugh.

"What's so funny?"

"Your face, dude. Seriously, you're hilarious."

"Shut up."

"Okay. I have an idea I've been wanting to run by you for a while and now seems like perfect timing."

"I'm listening."

"How about you just let her go?"

"Let her go? Why the hell would I do that?"

"Oliver, I mean come on, she lives all the way across the country. You won't call her. You won't write to her. And when you see her, you can't even mount up the courage to go talk to her. Maybe this is just a sign that the both of you should just move on with your own lives."

I frowned at him.

"And face it, dude, if you took a second to listen to yourself, and what you've been complaining about ever since you came back, *she* looks like she's doing exactly that."

I stood, walked over to my night table and grabbed the Christmas gift from Abby. It was the most thoughtful thing she could have ever gotten me: a digital camera filled with pictures. She wrote on the card she sent with the gift that everyone had passed around the camera. Anyone in school who wanted to pose, ended up with a picture on the camera. There were many pictures of her. I could tell that some of them were taken while she was posing, but the ones where she wasn't, were the most perfect ones.

I searched for my favorite one, it was a close up of Abby's face at the pond. Her crystal blue eyes told me how sad she was, but it was the most beautiful picture of her I had ever seen.

I handed my camera to my idiot friend. "Kayden, I'd like you to meet Abbygail Evens."

He let go of the remote and took the camera out of my hands. I watched his face as he took in Abby's picture. His stunned expression was enough for me to know what he thought, but I decided to ask anyway.

"So?"

"Shit Ol, she's fucking gorgeous."

"I know. Now please tell me, do you still think I should let her go?

He looked at me, unable to formulate a logic response.

"Yeah. That's what I thought."

"Oliver?" my mom yelled. "I'm home."

I stepped out from my room to greet her from her day at work. "How was your day?"

"Long. Did you cook the pasta like I asked?"

"Yes. It's in the oven and it should be ready in about ten minutes. Hey, Mom, can Kayden stay over for dinner?"

"Sure. Hi Kayden."

"Hi, Mrs. Langton."

"Oh, Oliver, I picked up the mail. Here, Abby sent you another letter."

Aw, fuck.

I'm not going to say hi.
I'm not even going to ask you how you are.
Because guess what? I don't care. But do you know what I do care about?
Us.
But apparently, I'm the only one. So, here's the deal.
I'm fucking pissed at you Oliver.
YOU CAME FOR X-MAS?!
You flew all the way across the country for two days, but couldn't find the time to come and see me. How could you?
Wait. Was that you I saw walking down our street?
UGH I'm so fucking confused right now... I hate that you're doing this to us, Oliver. IT HURTS.
How could you go see Stephan and Kylie, but not me?
Let's disregard my mom for a second, because she's one of the last people I want to talk about right now, I am way beyond pissed off at her... I'm not even sure I'll ever forgive her
Let's talk about our friends. My friends. You do understand that Kylie will tell me everything even though you ask her not to, right?
This isn't fair Oliver.

What have I done? Just tell me, so I know how to make things right.
And if you don't want me in your life anymore...
Tell me. That way I'll know and stop trying.
Abby.

CHAPTER TWENTY-SIX

ABBYGAIL

Five months.

Five long months without hearing anything from him.

Five months is nothing compared to sixteen years, but it's enough to break my heart.

I can't say I want to give up on our friendship because... well I can't. But the one thing I will do is stop waiting on him to love me because who am I kidding? I'm not getting anything back anyway.

Dear Oliver,
I'm still mad at you, but you're my friend and
friends don't give up on each other when things get
tough, so this is me trying. Again.

I miss you. How are you? How's school? Did you like the Christmas gift? I know it was a bit cheesy, but I figured it would be something you'd like.

How's your mom? Can you tell her I miss her please? I try to take as much news as I can from my mom, but she's being pretty scarce about anything that concerns you two ever since I threw a fit at her for not telling me she was having lunch with you at Rington's.

In case you were wondering, I'm doing okay. Between school, homework and babysitting, my days are pretty busy. My mom even agreed to let me take my driver's license exam, so I'm pretty stoked.

Zack and Adalynn are dating now, not that I care much. The only thing that pleases me by the news it is the fact that he'll finally get off my back about going out with him. He's the only one who was against respecting that stupid rule of yours, yet he was the only one I wish stuck with it. At least Stephan managed to get him off my back... finally.

Oh yeah, I almost forgot to tell you... do you remember Chase? His parents bought your house. Anyway, he asked me out. Turns out the Langton threat doesn't work on newcomers. So, ha, ha! Anyway, he wanted to take me to the Valentine's Day dance at school, but since I had already agreed to go with Tyler, I said no. But I'm pretty sure he'll try again. I'm pretty excited about it. He's pretty sweet. We've been hanging out a lot more since Christmas. I even stay over and have dinner with him a couple of times a week when he comes back from basketball practice. He's a bit older than us though. He's finishing high school this year.

Anyway, like I said he's pretty cool. I like him, and I'm pretty sure you'd like him too. He said he can't wait to meet you, so maybe next time you come home we could go out together. I really like him Oliver...

So, I know I've asked you this before, but I don't care if I repeat myself. Are you still mad at me? Why aren't you giving me any news Oliver? It's been five months already...

Is it because you're too busy?

Is it because you don't care?

I miss you. I miss us.

Just... give me something. Please!

I love you

Abby

Xxx

CHAPTER TWENTY-SEVEN

ABBYGAIL

"He's a prick." I complained to Chase as we made our way to my regular lunch table. I took a look outside as I walked through the doors of our smelly cafeteria, the wind was blowing snow in every possible direction. I was glad to be inside, the storm looked horrible and I could only hope it would be over by the time school was out.

"Who's a prick?" Kylie asked.

"Camdon."

"The gym teacher isn't a prick, Abs," Zoey interjected. "He's hot. It excuses his harsh behavior."

"It does not," I replied. "And just to make myself clear, he *was* hot. Now he's just a stupid teacher that wants us to do lay-ups until our legs aren't able to carry us anymore. Plus," I whined. "They're never good enough according to him."

"Maybe you're just not doing them right," Stephan teased.

"Maybe you should just shut up," I fired back.

Chase chuckled and kissed my cheek. "How about I give you private lessons after school tomorrow?"

"Why would I want private lessons? Playing basketball requires using a ball. I hate balls."

Stephan burst out laughing. "You hate balls? Okay, now I have to ask: what type of balls are you talking about exactly?"

"You're an idiot. And I'm going to hate *your* balls if you don't stop mocking me."

"You can hate my balls all you want, Babe, but I need to remind you that you need them to kick your ass during our training sessions."

"*Right*... now please remind me, why do I not hate them already?" I threw an evil smile and he returned the favor. I returned my attention to Chase who was leaning in for another kiss. He was always over-affectionate when we were around my friends. "So, about those private lessons?"

"Yeah?" he mumbled against my jaw.

I pulled back slightly to look at his hazel eyes. "Will you guarantee me an A?"

He rolled his eyes at me and returned to the crook

of my neck. "What I'll guarantee, Abby, is fun, body contact, sweat and a lot of kissing."

"Well I don't know, Chase," I replied. "I was *really* hoping for an A."

He slapped my ass and took a seat beside Tyler who was eying us quietly. I met his stare. I had no idea what was eating him up, but I wasn't going to let myself be intimidated by him.

"Have any of you thought about what we should get Oliver for his birthday?" I asked still standing at the head of the table.

"Again with Oliver... really, Abby? I mean come on, isn't this story over already?" I frowned at Zoey, not quite understanding where her attitude had come from. "Get a clue, Abs. He isn't calling you, he isn't sending you gifts, and I'm pretty sure he hasn't even written to you once. He came back for Christmas and didn't even stop by to say hi. For crying out loud, he's gone, Abs—"

"Enough, Zoey," Stephan snapped before I had a chance to reply.

"Come on, Steph, you have to agree with me on this." She glanced my way. "Sweetie, you need to get over him and move on."

"Zoey, I said that's enough."

"You have a boyfriend now." she continued, ignoring Stephan's demand. "How does Chase feel about your never-ending love for super-hot Oliver?"

I pulled my eyes away from Zoey and saw Chase's questioning stare. As if things couldn't be more humiliating...

He has lunch with us once a week and this conversation has to happen today? Why is she doing this to me?

"Zoey, Oliver is my friend. And for some reason, there's a concept you can't seem to grasp about friendship: people that care for each other, stick up for each other. Friends are supposed to support one another, regardless of time, distance, or anger." She flinched under my harsh tone. "And maybe you're right. Things between him and I have changed. And maybe at some point throughout our friendship my feelings for him have evolved, but you have no say in them and you have no right to judge them. Whatever I feel for Oliver has nothing to do with you. It's between us."

"But he's gone, Abby."

"Don't you think I fucking know? Because trust me, I do. It hurts *every time* I think about it—about him. But here's something you don't know. Even if he's gone, I still love him. I will always love him. He might live across the country, but he's still my best friend and I will stop trying to be his friend the day he tells me to stop and to back off." I could feel the tears threatening to fall. The fear of him telling me he wanted to end our friendship tore me apart. "But do you know what I don't get? Why do you even care?"

"I care because I'm worried. You've been miserable for six months, Abby. I just want what's best for you."

"If you want what's best for me, Zoey, then back the fuck off. This is my life. Let me live it the way I want."

"Abby." I looked up to Ava calling my name. She had a saddened expression on her face. Ava hated when Zoey and I argued, but it was when I noticed Chase walking out the cafeteria that I realized what she was trying to tell me.

"This is your fault," I snapped at Zoey.

"Don't blame this on me," she jeered. "You're the one that's in love with a guy but dating another."

"Fuck you."

I stormed out of the cafeteria looking for Chase. Luckily for me, he hadn't gotten very far: he was sitting on the wooden bench outside. It was still pretty windy, but at least the snow-fall had died down a little. I picked up my coat from my locker and went out to join him.

"Hey," I offered, stepping outside. I felt the shivers running down my spine, though I wasn't sure which storm I was mostly afraid to confront. "Can we talk?"

He moved over so I could sit by his side.

"Chase—"

"You never told me you were in love with him."

I tried to reply but he cut me off before I could.

"I had my doubts, though. There's always

something in your eyes when you talk about him. It's like they change color or something. I guess part of me didn't want to believe that you were in love with him as well."

"As well? What are you talking about?"

He let out a low sarcastic chuckle. "That's not quite the answer I was looking for."

"Chase," I stuttered.

"I guess the rumors were right on both parts."

"What rumors? What parts?"

"Abby, Oliver has the whole male student body under order that they are not to date you."

"It's a stupid joke, Chase. You don't know him. You don't know us. Oliver and I have been friends ever since we've been in diapers He did it to protect me from getting hurt."

"He did it because he's in love with you."

"Oliver is not in love with me." I replied confidently.

"Really? Funny how everyone that saw you walk out on him at homecoming dance last fall, doesn't seem to share the same opinion as you do. And let's not forget about Adalynn saying that she saw you two pretty hot and heavy in the girl's locker room."

I had overheard Adalynn talking about her walking in on us, but I never truly paid attention to what she had to say. I also never gave her the satisfaction of reacting to any of her blabbing. Adalynn's jealousy toward my relationship with Oliver was old news, but now that Chase had brought it up, I was starting to wonder if she really had seen what had happened between Oliver and me.

"If it isn't love, what is it?"

"I–" I teared up. I hadn't allowed myself to think about that night ever since I confronted Oliver about it. I didn't know how it happened, nor did I know why. "I don't know."

"Then maybe you should ask him."

I fucking tried that already...

"Do you love him?"

"I moved on."

"That wasn't my question."

"Chase. I don't know. I don't know what you want me to say."

"Just answer the damn question, Abbygail. It isn't that hard of a question." His voice softened. "I like you, Abby. I *really* like you but—"

"I like you too. Please don't turn this into something it's not."

He stood. "Then answer the question. Are you or are you not still in love with him?"

My eyes fell to the ground. I was unable to give him the answer he wanted to hear.

He stepped closer to me, lifted my head to meet his eyes and wiped my overflowing tears. "Abby, I want this to work, but the fact that you are unable to answer me should be a clue for you. I don't think you worked through whatever feelings you had *or* have for this guy." He exhaled loudly. "I don't want to be your rebound guy, Abs. I want to be *the* guy. Please let me know when you figure this out. Okay?"

I nodded and watched Chase walk away from me with his hands in his pockets until all I could see was the shadow of his back behind the wall of blowing snow.

CHAPTER TWENTY-EIGHT

OLIVER

Abby was right. Celebrating my birthday without my best friend for the first time in my life was beyond weird. It wasn't bad; it just wasn't what it was supposed to be. My evening started with a trip to the tattoo parlor with my mother: she and I had gotten into a discussion about my birthday gift at least three weeks before, and I always came back with the same response: I wanted a tattoo. That was it. I even told her I would pay for it. All she needed to do was to come to the parlor with me and give the guy her authorization since I wasn't of age.

I was ecstatic when she agreed.

The tattoo I chose was huge, and the hours I spent with my back to the table while I got it, hurt like hell.

But it was a different kind of pain, a comforting pain. When I stepped off his station and saw the result, I decided that the suffering I had gone through was totally worth it. My mother on the other hand didn't agree. When she came back to pick me up a few hours later and saw the art on my chest, she flipped. She was angry with my decision and made sure I understood that I would spend my life regretting my lack of judgement.

She knew nothing.

I got dressed and as I took a last look at my reflection in the mirror, I knew that this guy's designs on my body would be one of many. I loved the experience and the artist's work.

Eighteen isn't that far, I'll be back soon enough.

After a night out with my friends I came back and found Abby's letter sitting on my pillow. I smiled. I liked how she always found a way for me to receive her letters whenever I needed them the most. It might not have been perfect, because perfect would have been finding *her* sitting on my pillow, but it definitely made up for her absence.

I opened the thick letter and pulled out a leather bracelet. Abby had a fascination about working with leather. She started the whole thing after coming back from a day at the flea market with my mom and had continued with her passion ever since.

As I paid attention to every carved detail and

design, I noticed how talented she'd become over the last few months and wrapped the bracelet around my wrist.

It fit perfectly and I loved it.

Hey Oliver,

If I calculated this right, you're 17 now. Happy birthday!!! How does it feel to still be younger than me by 4 months? Ha! I was right, this will never get old.

I hope you like your gift. It's not exactly what I wanted it to be, but things got out of hand at school last Friday and, well, some of us aren't really on speaking terms right now. By some of us, I mean Zoey and me. Also, Tyler, for some reason he won't talk to me either. I'm not quite sure what ran up his ass, but honestly, right now, I don't really care. Well, not enough to ask...

Anyway, you'll be proud, I was so pissed off at Zoey and everything else about my crappy life that I left school and I skipped an entire afternoon of class for the first time of my life. My mother on the other hand is pretty pissed off at me. I'm grounded, obviously.

Ever had a week where your whole life feels like it's falling to pieces? Because that's how mine is going right now... although according to Zoey, it's been the story of my last six months. She says I'm too hung up on you and that if I meant anything to you, you would have written back or come to see me during the holidays. She wants me to move on and disregard our friendship as if it was nothing. She doesn't get it... but what's worse is that she threw her fit right in the middle of the cafeteria, in front of all our friends and Chase, who by the way has lunch with me once a week. I don't get it. How can she think like that? How can she possibly believe that I'll just disregard sixteen years of friendship as if it was nothing?

But then a part of me keeps wondering if maybe she's right...

Everything is screwed up.

I screwed up.

I'm pretty sure Chase and I are over.

I must have the crappiest dating record on earth. I'm seventeen years old and I finally have a boyfriend, but end up ruining it within two weeks because of Zoey's big mouth.

Oliver, I'd give anything to hear your voice or have you hold my hand right now. I miss how you always find a way to make me laugh when I'm pissed off or how you're able to make me think and see things more clearly. I miss you, Oliver. More than you could possibly believe.

Could you just please call, or write, or text, or something?

Please?

Abby

xxx

I don't know what I yelled that had my mother shouting my name from her bedroom across the house, but when she opened the door she was clearly bothered by my demeanor. I looked at the time and winced, it was past midnight.

"I'm sorry."

"Are you okay? What's the matter with you?"

"Nothing. I'm sorry," I replied both regretful and angry.

"How was your night?"

"It was great, until ten minutes ago."

She frowned and looked at Abby's letter that was sitting at my feet. She took a step closer and noticed the leather bracelet on my wrist.

"It's pretty. Did she make it?"

"Uh huh."

"Wow. She's getting pretty good at this, isn't she? So, how is our dear Abbygail?"

I took the bracelet off and threw it at the end of the bed. "She has a new boyfriend."

"I see." She picked up Abby's gift and placed it on my dresser. "Do you want to talk about it?"

"No."

She sighed. "So, tell me Oliver. How's your tattoo this evening?"

I rolled my eyes. It was as if she knew the whole thing would be blowing up in my face sooner rather than later and enjoyed rubbing it in my face. "It hurts. Is that what you wanted to hear?"

"No. But then again, I did warn you it would."

I frowned, but replied nothing.

"If you change your mind about talking, come and see me."

I won't. I'm done. With all of it.

"You wanted me to say something," I mumbled to myself. I grabbed the pen and paper inside my night table. "This is me saying something."

CHAPTER TWENTY-NINE

OLIVER

I never sent Abby my letter. I sent hers back, as I normally did, but mine stayed on my desk for almost a week. It taunted me day and night while I debated whether I should be mailing it or not, and on the fourth day I realized that I couldn't do it.

When I walked into my house after school, it was spotless. My mother either went through a cleaning fit or a high emotional breakdown, and my guess was the latter because she had been acting weirdly ever since my outburst over the weekend.

"Mom?" I called out to her as I passed by the kitchen to grab a snack.

"I'm in your room, sweetheart."

I grimaced. Having her include my room in her

cleaning ritual meant that she was really having a bad day. I opened the door, and sure enough, it was clean–too clean. She was standing by the window, still in her pyjamas, looking out at the mountain-side. She looked broken and exhausted.

"Mom, what's wrong?"

"Nothing," she sniffed.

She was about to cry, so I walked over to her and drew her into a warm hug. "Do you want to talk about it?"

Probably remembering the line she had said to me only a few days before, she lifted her head off my shoulder. "Cute. But it's nothing. I just really miss your father today."

I didn't reply. I completely understood how she felt. When it came to my father, some days were just harder than others. After a few minutes of embracing, she sighed, and pulled away.

"Do you know how much I love you?"

"I have a feeling, but I'm not that sure," I teased. "How about you show me by taking me out for dinner tonight?"

She laughed. "I truly hope you won't be using that line on a girl one day."

"If I do, I'll let you know how it goes."

"Please do. So, what kind of food were you thinking?"

"Oh, I don't know, I was thinking sushi might be good. What do you think?"

"I think you're trying to please your mother rather than please yourself."

She was right. I didn't really like sushi. In fact, I wasn't a fan Asian food at all.

"What can I say? I'm just awesome like that."

Her tender eyes met mine. "Give me twenty minutes, and I'll be ready."

The need to destroy Abby's letter never felt as strong as it did at that exact moment. As soon as my mother stepped out, I went straight to my desk. Unfortunately, the letter wasn't there. It wasn't on my night table, on the floor or under my bed. I searched in every drawer, even in the garbage: it wasn't there. It wasn't anywhere.

"Mom?" I panicked. "When you cleaned up my room did you see the envelope on my desk addressed to Abby?"

"Yes."

I exhaled in relief.

"Where did you put it?"

"I mailed it. The postman was delivering our mail when I was taking the trash out this morning. I handed it to him instead of having to walk down the hill to the mail box."

"So, it's gone?"

"Yep."

I paled.

"I was so happy to see you had written to her. I figured that since it was just lying around I'd mail it for you. I hope it was okay."

I didn't answer. I just backed away from my door and sat on my bed.

I think I'm going to throw up...

CHAPTER THIRTY

ABBYGAIL

C hase and I walked home from the bus drop off
side-by-side without addressing each other. I
couldn't even say if we were a couple or not anymore,
but my guess was that we weren't because we hadn't
really talked since our fallout at school. I wished there
was something I could say, but there wasn't. He was
right. Zoey was right. Even though I hadn't heard
anything from Oliver in nearly six months, even
though he was hurting me beyond repair, I was still
very much in love with my best friend.

I spotted my mother rolling into our driveway
when we rounded the corner. The weather station had
predicted some freezing rain, which was probably why
she made it home earlier than usual. The wind had

picked up about an hour before school ended, blowing in the heavy low clouds that were threatening to burst over our heads at any moment. I was glad to see her step out of the car when I made it to my house, greeting her made leaving Chase at the curb without saying goodbye, less awkward.

"Hi, Mom."

"Hey, Sweetheart. Hi, Chase."

I turned to see him answering her with a tight smile.

"I see your issues with him haven't been resolved yet," she whispered for only me to hear.

I shrugged in response.

"I really wish the both of you could talk this out." My mother liked Chase, which was weird since she normally didn't like me hanging me out with older guys. Although, I think she preferred the shift in my mood when he was around rather than the relationship itself.

She reached inside the mailbox and pulled out a pile of envelopes while I observed Chase walk inside his house. As soon as his door shut, I turned my focus back to her. "How was your day?"

"I was pretty busy this morning, but things died down in the afternoon. All of my customers cancelled their appointments because of the freezing rain forecast. So, what are your plans for tonight?" My mother asked while her busy hands rummaged through the pile of letters.

We walked inside our house together, and I dropped my bag on the floor with a loud thud. The quantity of homework I had was ridiculous. "I might invite Stephan over to watch a movie if it's okay with you."

My mother dangled an envelope in my face.

"What?"

"It's for you."

"Who's it from?" I took off my laced combat boots and hung my coat in the closet frowning. The only mail I normally received was my monthly subscription to Seventeen Magazine.

"It doesn't say. There is no return address."

I took the envelope from her hands and smiled.

"You seem pleased."

I nodded. "It's from Oliver."

"Really?"

I climbed the three steps to the main floor. There was something in the way she answered that rubbed me the wrong way. "Why do you seem so surprised?"

"I'm not," she mumbled. "I was just thinking about a thing I forgot at work."

My brows pinched, she was lying. I was about to call her out on it, but the lights of our house flashed and it distracted me. We both looked outside, catching a glimpse of the weather. Through the kitchen window I saw that the wind had picked up a vigorous speed, swinging the branches of the willow tree in every direction. "I'm going to go read this in my room, okay?"

"Sure, go ahead. Let me know if Stephan will be coming for dinner or not."

Dear Abbygail,

I'm sorry about you and Zoey, but I wouldn't worry too much about it. You know how you two are, and I'm sure things will get better in no time. I would even bet a root beer slushy on it.

But the thing is, Abby, Zoey is right. There is a reason why I'm not writing back. Do you remember when I told you I didn't care what you had to say to prevent me from leaving? I didn't care because it was my decision to leave.

I told you I wanted you to let me go and I left because I wanted out.

I wanted out of our school. Out of my home. Out of our town.

Abbygail, I wanted out of us.

I know what you're trying to do by writing to me all the time, and I want you to stop. Can't you see that this isn't working for you? How many letters have you written that I haven't replied to?

I don't want you to be a part of my life anymore. I

want you to move on with your life, but I especially need you to let me move on with mine.

Besides, my girlfriend Laney doesn't like you writing to me all the time. Every time you send something, your letter becomes a source of conflict. She gets jealous even though I keep telling her that you're just an old friend.

She's pretty cool though, and fucking hot too. Look her up on Facebook. Her name is Laney Benton. You'll see she's awesome. I'm sure you'd love her just as much as I do or as much as you think I'd like the next-door neighbor who you're supposed to be dating.

I moved on Abs, I have a great life in BC. I have great friends, I'm doing well in school, my house is awesome, I'm playing football...my life is better than it was. I'm completely over my life in Carrington; I don't miss anything from home.

So, how about we keep what we had a great memory and move on, okay?

I need you to let go now. It's just better this way, for the both of us.

Abbygail, just...

Don't ever let the orchids fade away.

Oliver

My name was being called from behind. I frowned,

looked behind me and saw Stephan standing in my doorway with worry.

"Abby?" My mother called again. Both were observing me sitting on the floor in the middle of piles of pictures and destroyed property: mine and Oliver's property.

I had absolutely no idea how everything had happened, but my body was shaking uncontrollably. My brows furrowed as I tried to figure out what was going on. Nothing made sense until I glanced down and saw his letter resting on my lap.

A loud cry escaped me. Raw anger. Agonizing, throbbing pain.

Oliver had done exactly what he promised me he'd never do. I didn't want to cry anymore. Tried to stop it, but my heart betrayed me.

A hot tear rolled down my cheek as I stood. "Mom. I am going for a run."

I left my house without looking back. I ran until I couldn't catch my breath anymore and then pushed harder just because I could.

I choked on every inhale, stifled on every exhale.

My heart throbbed with every step.

The drops of freezing rain hitting my face felt like a thousand needles painfully piercing my skin at the same time.

I welcomed the pain.

I didn't notice the water and ice accumulation. The

splash of my running shoes hitting the frozen wet pavement didn't bother me until I lost my footing and fell to the ground.

I tried to get up, but the sharp throb around my left ankle prevented me from standing.

Everything... everything just—

I prayed for the oncoming car to swerve and hit me, but it didn't. It stopped. The driver didn't continue on his merry way, he opened the door, picked me up and brought me home.

As for the heartbreak that Oliver's betrayal inflicted on me, it didn't die... it didn't disappear.

But then deep down, I knew it never would.

CHAPTER THIRTY-ONE

OLIVER

I held the letter in my hands. I had already read it once, but as if my heart couldn't believe she had given up on us, I read it again, and again.

And then, because I knew that I was holding in my hand the remainder of her tears for our friendship, I mixed my own with hers, one last time.

Dear Oliver,

I have this vague memory of us sitting on your front porch. I think it was after my eighth birthday party, or maybe it was before... I don't know. But who cares because it's beyond the point anyway. The point is that I turned eight years old that day and life had given me the best gift I could possibly wish for.

It gave me a best friend.

It gave me you.

You held me while I cried because even though I rarely talked about him, you knew that Simon leaving me hurt me every day. That birthday was the last time we spoke of him. That birthday was the day you told me that you would share your dad with me.

Do you remember that day Oliver? I do... for so many reasons, too. You gave me my first orchid that day. It was white and blue. It was perfect. It was the first time I'd seen one, yet it instantly became my favorite flower.

But you know what else that day was Oliver? That day was when you told me that I was your best friend. You told me you would never leave me. That day you promised me you would never hurt me.

I believed you. I trusted you.

Seventeen years...

Oliver, when you left, I never questioned our friendship. I knew that if anything bad was to happen to me, you would be on the next flight home, no questions asked. It's who we are, Oliver. It's who we have always been. Or so I thought...

I'm sorry I inconvenienced you so much. I thought our friendship meant more to you. I thought I meant more to you... but I guess I was wrong.

Oliver, whatever you set out to do when you wrote to

me, <u>for the first time in six months</u>, you've succeeded. You destroyed whatever friendship we had left and you shredded my heart along with it.

You have never purposefully hurt me until now. Not only did you abandon me; you broke your promise. You didn't hurt me, Oliver. You shattered me. You're not just as bad as Simon was, YOU'RE worse.

I hate you. I don't think I've ever hated someone as much as I hate you. Fuck you, and fuck your memories.

I <u>don't</u> want them to linger.

I want to forget about them.

I want to forget about you.

I never ever want to see you or hear your name ever again.

Have a great life.

Or don't, I don't care.

Abbygail Evens

P.S. She looks like a blond bimbo. Not your type... well that's what you always said anyway. But then again, our entire friendship was a lie. So what do I know?

CHAPTER THIRTY-TWO

THREE MONTHS LATER

ABBYGAIL

S itting on the ground with my head resting on the player's bench, I breathed in the soundless breeze passing through the football field. The night was clear of clouds, but unexpectedly cool for the first day of summer.

School was officially over. How I managed to pass tenth grade was beyond me. I don't think I could recall anything I'd learned over the school year. According to the teachers, though, I apparently had retained sufficient information for me to move on to the next step. I was moving on to eleventh grade, one step closer to the end of high school.

One step closer to not knowing what the hell I'm going to do with my life... not that I care.

I laughed bitterly at myself, and took another swig at the bottle I was holding in my hand. Tequila was a hypocritical drink, but I loved how the buzz of too many consecutive shots hit me unexpectedly.

"Hello there, Abbygail." It came from few feet behind me, but I didn't need to turn around to know who it was. I'd recognize the smooth sound of his deep voice anytime.

"Hello, Damian."

The entire concept of fleeing the end of year celebration I was supposed to be attending, was to avoid talking with anyone. I wanted to be alone. My appearance at the party lasted a total of one and a half hours before I decided to bail. It was just enough time for my friends to notice me making an effort, but not too long for me to get bored. It was also just long enough for me to snatch the poor bottle of tequila just sitting there alone on our host's kitchen counter without being noticed.

I swallowed another gulp and grimaced as I felt the burn traveling down my throat. But it wasn't the strong taste of the alcohol that bothered me, it was the unpredicted arrival of the guy climbing the fence behind the bleachers.

Damian Bushmans was bad for me.

"Did you keep some for me?" he asked, as he got closer to where I was sitting.

Damian was hot. He was the kind of guy girls

lusted over even though they knew they shouldn't get close because he would be bad for them. He was tall, well built, with short sandy blond hair and baby blue eyes. He had the perfect boy-next-door look, but he was so far from being one.

I handed him the bottle and he sat further down the bench taking a gulp of his own. "So, Abbygail. I haven't seen you here in a while. What's got you wallowing here all alone?"

"I doubt you've ever seen me here at all, Damian."

"Why would you say that?"

"Right off the top of my head? Because you're not the football kind of guy."

"And how would you know? I don't really like when people make blind assumptions about me, Abbygail. You do know I hang out with Liam, don't you?"

I sat up to join him on the bench and put my legs up facing him. "So? Just because your friends with the quarterback I'm supposed to guess that you watch him play?"

"You shouldn't suppose anything at all," he replied after swallowing another mouthful. He handed me my bottle back, but still didn't look at me. "You should ask. And for the record, he is my best friend."

"So?"

He finally directed his attention to me. "Well if I recall things correctly, no less than a year ago you were here on a daily basis encouraging your best friend."

"How would you know that?"

"Just because you don't see me, doesn't mean I don't see you."

I rolled my eyes. "Great, I now have my own personal stalker."

He laid his back on the bench and looked up at the sky. "Don't flatter yourself. I'm just saying that you shouldn't judge a book by its cover."

"Trust me, I'm not judging you by your cover. I know who you are, Damian Bushmans."

"Really?" He lifted his head to look at me for barely a second and then settled it back down. "You just titillated my curiosity, Ms. Evens. Please tell me. Who am I?"

"You're the guy that drove my best friend away from me."

He chuckled. If I'd had enough strength, I would have gotten up and punched him in the face. Unfortunately, with the amount of alcohol streaming through my blood it wouldn't have resulted in anything remotely painful. So instead of looking like a fool with a pretend punch, I stayed still and pushed the thought of the guy that left me behind as far down as I could.

The last thing I wanted to feel were tears forming in my eyes.

"I didn't drive Oliver away from you. He was just strong enough to leave before being dragged down with what I had to offer."

I tightened my fists and dug my nails inside the palm of my hands. "I don't want to talk about him."

"You're the one that brought him up."

"And I'm the one telling you I don't want to talk about him." I grinded my teeth. "Why are you here, Damian?"

"I saw you cross the street, and you looked like you needed the company. My good nature was telling me I should come and see if you were okay."

"Your good nature? You don't even like me."

"There you go assuming things again, Abbygail. Didn't I just tell you that you shouldn't do that?" The way he said my name made me shiver. It was sexy, yet the danger in it was clearly apparent. He reached inside his leather jacket, and pulled out what looked like a cigarette and lit up beside me.

The strong smell piqued my curiosity. I could only make out the silhouette of Damian's face as he took in a deep breath. I watched him smoke quietly and admired his square jaw through the soft glow of the moonlight. After a while of my staring at him, he lifted his head and his serious lips turned into a sexy grin.

"What?"

"I just wonder why you do it."

He smirked. "Why do I do what?"

"The drugs."

"You want to know why I use or why I sell?" he asked, admiring the sky.

I followed his gaze. "Both. I guess."

"I use because it feels good and helps keep my mind off the shit going on in my life. I sell because I need the money."

"Why do you need the money?"

"Because my father's an ass and I need to eat and drink just like you do. Plus, this hot bod isn't going to dress itself you know."

"Hot bod?" I snorted. "You're so full of shit, Bushmans."

"Are you telling me you don't think I'm hot?"

"That's exactly what I'm saying."

He sat up and moved closer to me. I felt his long gaze trailing up and down my body, and after sizing me up he chuckled and licked his lips. "Funny how your eyes seem to tell an entirely different story."

"Why don't you just get a real job like everyone else does?" I asked, trying to get the attention off me and my obvious attraction towards him.

"Why would I? It's easy money. Besides, I'm good at what I do."

I remained quiet, pensive for a while. Damian was extremely smart, and I had to admit; he ran his business very well. But even I knew selling drugs was a stupid idea. "You're going to get caught some day."

"I'll cross that bridge if I get there."

"You mean when."

Just as if he knew I was right and that his time would come soon, he let out a deep sexy laugh that made my insides quiver.

I stretched my hand, and grazing my fingers against his, I took the lit joint. After looking at it for what seemed like an eternity I put the moist tip on my lips and sucked in sharply, swallowing the strong smoke down my constricted lungs. I choked and coughed my life away, and all Damian did was let his head fall back as he exploded into a fit laughter.

"Fuck you." I managed to complain between coughs. "You could have warned me."

"I'm glad I didn't. This has got to be the funniest thing I've seen all day. You're a lousy smoker, Abbygail."

I rolled my eyes, annoyed. "Okay, Damian, since you seem to think you are such an expert, how about you show me how it's supposed to be done?"

"Gladly." He moved even closer to me and placed his legs on each side of the bench we were sitting on, and demanded I do the same.

I let my legs down and straddled it just as he did. Deep down, his nearness was scaring me: I knew I shouldn't be sitting there with Damian. He gave Oliver the drugs… he made Oliver leave me. He was my enemy, yet I was unable to back away.

My inhibited self was kicking me in the gut because not only did I not want to leave, I was enjoying his company. I wanted to be with him.

"Close your eyes and open your mouth."

I frowned at his request. It was the type of thing Henry would say when I'd surprise him with my usual pre-diner visit.

ONE YEAR AGO

"Hi, Uncle Henry," I hollered, walking through the front door without knocking.

"Hey, Abbygail. How was your day?" He stretched his neck from the kitchen. "Come take a seat, I'm making dinner."

I crossed the hallway and sat in front of him at the counter. I watched as he diced various types of vegetables in front of me. "It was okay, I guess. I had a French exam this morning."

"How did it go?"

"Honestly? I'm pretty sure I flunked it."

"I really doubt that. Isn't that the exam you and Oliver studied for all evening yesterday?"

I nodded but it was a lie. Oliver and I hadn't spent hours studying, we had spent hours watching deleted scenes of

'Dexter' online and then I spent the entire night awake because of it.

"You two were at it for hours. What happened?"

I shrugged and looked at my hands.

"I think you underestimate yourself, Abby. You're a lot better than you think. I wish you gave yourself more credit and believed in yourself more."

"Maybe." I frowned.

"Okay, what's the matter kid? This isn't about your French class is it?"

I shook my head. Bizarre feelings about my best friend were bubbling inside of me for the past months, and had no idea what to think of them. I needed to talk to someone and out of all the people surrounding me, the only person I could think of was my best friend's father.

Talk about awkward.

"Abbygail?"

"How did you know you were in love with Aunt Evelynn?"

He smiled and put his knife down on the cutting board. "Who's the lucky guy?"

I groaned. I knew the question would be coming up sooner than later. "No one. Forget I asked. So, what are you making for dinner tonight?"

He chuckled. "Why do I have a feeling that you're changing the subject because you don't want me to figure out who your secret crush is?"

"Oh, I'm well over the crush phase now. So, tell me. What are we having for dinner?"

He smiled. "Close your eyes and open your mouth."

"Hey Dad, I'm home."

I felt my heart thrumming at the sound of his voice and opened my eyes before the spoon touched my lips.

'We're in the kitchen. How was practice?" Henry replied to his son.

"It was okay. Coach made us do the beep test for over half an hour, though. It was fucking exhausting. Who's we?" he asked, climbing upstairs to his room before coming into the kitchen.

"It's either one of two people." I replied, hearing him run back down the steps. "I'll let you take a wild guess."

"Abs? I was just about to go knock on Cole's door. Weren't you supposed to be babysitting?"

"Mr. Hunter got home earlier. I came here to surprise you before you got home." I grinned at the drink he was holding in his hand when he walked in. "Is that for me?"

"Only if you agree to share." He kissed my cheek.

I hopped off the high chair I was sitting on, grabbed the spoon Henry was still holding out for me and popped it in my mouth. I moaned. It was delicious, as always.

"Am I keeping you a spot for dinner?" Henry asked, returning to his stove.

"I think that was already implied, Uncle Henry." I smiled and stepped out of the kitchen with Oliver. He and I would be crossing the street to go sit under the willow tree in my backyard to enjoy our frozen drink together.

"I guess it was. Tell your mom we're having you for diner and that if she wants to join us, she is more than welcome."

"Okay." I grabbed the glass out of Oliver's hands and took a huge gulp of the frozen drink. "Shit."

"Brain freeze?" Oliver teased.

I nodded.

"Where?"

I pointed to my forehead, and he hit me with the palm of his hand.

"Dude." I winced. "Why the hell did you do that?"

"It's a known fact that if you hit your head where your brain freezes it will make the pain disappear, Abby."

"But you just hit me, dimwit."

"Did the brain freeze go away?"

"Well yeah but—"

"Then don't complain." He snorted at the annoyed glare I show his way.

We started walking out of the front door when I heard Uncle Henry calling my name. I stopped and spun on my heels.

"I had trouble breathing when she wasn't there, Abby," he explained from the kitchen. "That's how I knew I would never be able to let her go, that's how I knew I would do anything for her, and that's how I knew I was in love with her."

I nodded and walked over to Oliver who was waiting for me leaning on the front door. "What the hell was that about?"

"Nothing" I looked at my Uncle Henry one last time before shutting the door behind me and saw him wink. I put my finger up to my lips: my secret was out, and bizarrely enough I was relieved.

"So, beautiful," Oliver put his arm around my shoulders. "How did your French exam go?"

I groaned.

"Yeah, me too. Next time we need to study, let's not watch 'Dexter.'"

"I had nightmares because of you. Weren't you supposed to come and sleep over last night?"

"I tried to sneak out, but my mom caught me." He reached for the glass I was indulging in. "Give me that before you drink it all."

"You want it?" I rushed out of his arms. "Come and get it."

Months before, I appreciated the random thoughts of Henry popping into my head, they made me smile. But as time moved forward, memories of Henry would turn into thoughts of Oliver, and I didn't welcome those as well as I used to.

Reminiscing about Oliver and how much I missed

him was heartwrenching. I preferred convincing myself that I hated him. It was just easier to push down the memories about us as far as I could and forget about them. Or him.

"I won't be putting anything disgusting in your mouth, Abbygail," Damian pointed out.

"Why should I trust you?"

He smiled. "You shouldn't, Little-Bird. I'm a predator. And little birds like you should never trust guys like me.

I don't trust you... I don't even trust myself right now...

"But in this case, I guess you're just going to need to believe me."

I watched Damian bring his lit joint to his mouth and breathe in the smoke. I licked my lips waiting to see what would happen next, and he smiled.

"Close your eyes and part your lips," he whispered as he inched closer to me. I followed his order and felt the warm smoke he slowly puffed from his mouth to mine.

I inhaled and let it travel down my throat. His proximity made my head dizzy and my heart race at an extremely fast pace. The experience was a thousand times better than it had been just seconds before. I swallowed the smoke down and let the air leave my lungs slowly. When I opened my eyes, Damian was staring at my mouth. I bit down on my lower lip.

"You shouldn't do that."

"I shouldn't do what?"

"Bite your lip like you keep doing *all the fucking time.*"

I giggled. "Why?"

"Because it makes me want to kiss you."

"Is that so?" I purred. "And tell me, Damian, what's stopping you from kissing me right now?"

He didn't respond with words.

As soon as his lips touched mine I lost myself. My will to fight, my will to be the person I knew I could be… it all disappeared to his greedy demanding kiss.

I loved the way his tongue grazed mine. I adored how his teeth bit into my bottom lip. The way he devoured my mouth and the side of my jaw, made my skin shiver. When he lifted me to straddle his hard body, I felt desired. The sound of his lustful moans made me feel wanted. His eager callous fingers skimming my body inside the protection of my clothing, caressing my scorching wet skin, made my heart race faster than it had in months.

I loved how Damian Bushmans made me feel alive.

But above all, what I loved the most was letting myself get lost to someone I really didn't care about.

CHAPTER THIRTY-THREE

ABBYGAIL

M y sleepy eyes tried to adjust to the harsh sunlight when I woke up. I couldn't understand why it was shining so bright in the morning.

Unless it's the afternoon and Mom let me sleep in?

I shook my head knowing that the probability of my mother letting me sleep until late afternoon was highly unlikely.

I sat up, feeling very dehydrated and reached to my side table, but my hand hit a wall that was normally not there. Feeling more than a little disoriented I rubbed my eyes and looked around; nothing in the room I was sitting in made sense.

What the hell happened last night?

Scratch that... where the hell am I?

As I tried to assess my surroundings, the door to my left opened and I saw him come in. "Damian? What are you doing here?"

"You're in *my* room, babe. Where else am I supposed to be?"

"Your room?" I frowned trying recall what had happened in the last few hours. The last thing I could recollect was us kissing, and him feeling me up on the football field's line-up bench.

I looked down. I was wearing his Vans T-shirt.

Shit.

"Yes, my room. How are you feeling? Do you have a headache?" His concern surprised me.

Unable to word anything that made sense, I licked my dried lips and shook my head.

"There's a glass of water on my side table if you want a drink."

I nodded, picked up the glass on the left side of the bed and brought it to my lips. The warm water going down my throat wasn't soothing much. "Can I—um—use your bathroom?"

He nodded, never letting his eyes falter away from mine. "Second door to your right."

I stepped out of Damian's room with wobbly legs, felt his gaze following me out, but I didn't dare look behind me. When I came back feeling a little fresher than I had a few minutes before, Damian was still standing at the exact same spot, waiting for me.

"Feeling better, Little-Bird?" A mocking smirk tugged at the corner of his lips. He took his shirt off and unbuckled his belt, letting his lose jeans hang low on his hips.

"Sort of. What time is it?"

He looked completely unphased by my studying the scars covering his chest. "Nine."

Okay, so my mom is definitely killing me now...

"Where are my clothes?" It had dawned on me when I got out of bed that I was wearing absolutely nothing under Damian's shirt. He didn't say a word, he only nudged towards the corner and I saw *all* my clothing neatly folded on his computer desk.

Really Abby?

"Last night, did we—um?"

He shook his head. "At some point you passed out."

I slipped back into Damian's bed covers and leaned on the wall behind me. Why I wasn't running out of his bedroom screaming my head off, I had no clue. In any normal circumstances I would have been out of the door, yet there I was taking back the spot I had woken up confused in, with absolutely no intention of leaving.

"Abbygail," Damian voiced. His low growl hadn't gone unnoticed.

I smiled. I watched him swallow the lump in his

throat when his eyes trailed down to the sight of his t-shirt running higher up my thighs.

"Damian," I murmured.

He raised his brow. "Tell me how you're feeling right now."

My eyes skimmed the length of his naked torso and stopped at the sight of his buldge. A sly smile crept up on me. "I'm just going to go ahead and say that I'm feeling exactly what you're feeling, Bushmans."

The fire in his gaze was questioning me. Warning me.

I didn't care.

Damian meant nothing and for the first time in my life I didn't give a shit about the consequences of my choices. What I cared about was my desire to feel his hands caressing my skin as they had on the football field the previous night. What I cared about was that he wouldn't be stopping there. He would take more because I wanted more. And if he requested it, I would give him all.

He unbuttoned his pants and they hit the floor letting his very present erection show me exactly how aroused he was. I licked my lips and he advanced towards me. "I want to try something with you, Little Bird."

"Could you please stop calling me that?" I complained.

"Nah! I don't think I will. I kind of like the nickname. It fits you." He climbed onto the bed, straddled my half naked body and reached inside his night table. I watched him pull out a condom and a bottle of pills. He uncapped the bottle, pulled a bright pink pill out, and bit into the tablet, splitting it in two.

My brows pinched. "What is it?"

"Ecstasy."

Ecstasy? Okay. That's not so bad right?

I wrapped my hands around his neck and put my lips to his. With an appreciative growl, he stroked his tongue with mine and slipped my half of the drug inside my mouth. I swallowed it down without giving another thought, and pulled his hard body down over mine.

"Abbygail?" he moaned against my jaw. "Did you know that I could barely sleep while you were rubbing your tight bare ass on my dick last night?"

"Well Damian," I replied, mocking him. "If you hadn't undressed me, then it wouldn't have been bare."

"I didn't undress you, Little-Bird, you undressed yourself. This shirt was the only thing you agreed to put on after I begged you to stay dressed."

I frowned a bit bothered by his admission. "Why did you want me dressed?"

"I'm a drug dealer, Abby. Not a rapist. If I'm going to have sex with you, you're going to be awake and I'm going to make sure you enjoy it." He lifted his shirt off my back and let in a sharp appreciative breath. I loved how he looked at me and worshiped my body with his eyes. "I also wanted to be sure that you understood what you were willing to give up last night, and that it was still what you wanted once you had a clear head."

His fingers caressed my skin until they reached the inside of my wet thighs. I moaned, pleasured by his skilled touch, and he put his lips back on mine.

My skin tingled. Every nerve in my body was in overdrive. Every touch of his hand, lips and tongue felt like fireworks of pure pleasure bursting inside of me.

"Are you sure about this?" he asked, grazing my entrance.

I closed my eyes and saw the dark pair of eyes I missed so much staring angrily at me.

Ignore them, Abby. He left you.

I lifted my hips and guided Damian slowly inside of me.

His thrusts were long and greedy, pounding unapologetically in and out of me.

He took what he wanted and gave me what I needed.

He's gone. And so are you...

CHAPTER THIRTY-FOUR

FIVE YEARS AND SEVEN MONTHS LATER

OLIVER

"Will I be seeing you tonight?" she asked as we walked down the cream-colored halls of my house. She and I had been together a little over a month, but honestly our relationship was mostly based on physical attraction. She was pretty with long brown hair, big brown eyes and an amazing body I craved to get myself lost in. But the thing about Sam was that regardless of the fact that my mother's sickness was getting worse by the day, she was very adamant about spending every free moment in my company.

It annoyed the hell out of me.

"I don't know, Sam. I'll see how my mom's doing later in the day, and give you a call."

"Oliver?" I heard my mother calling me again from her room. I could only hope she hadn't been calling me for too long.

"I'll be right there, Mom."

When high school ended, I moved out of my mother's house and found an apartment in Surrey, with my friends Kayden and Laney. Laney studied health and became a nurse, Kayden studied business, hoping to become a renowned business consultant, and studied social services.

About a year before earning my degree, I noticed that every time I saw her, my mother was losing weight. Her skin-tone was pale, she slept a lot, and even though she had many hours of sleep, she always complained about feeling weak. It was weird. My mother had always been full of energy and joy, her frail state bothered me. Finally, after weeks of arguing with her, I managed to convince her to let my Uncle Jerry take her to see her doctor. It turned out she had bone cancer.

The blow shattered my world. I felt helpless and was ready to give everything up in order to help. Unfortunately, my mother had refused to let me quit school so I could take care of her. She and I had gotten into it more times than I could count. I hated not being there for her. I hated that every time I saw her she looked worse than the last. But that's what cancer was all about and I had no other choice but comply with her desires.

So, while I was in school, my uncle took care of her and whenever I could, I would go back home and take over. It involved a lot of travelling, but it was the only way. I earned my degree exactly like she demanded I do, and came back to live with her second I was done.

"Listen, Oliver, I get it. She's sick. But don't you think you're allowed to have a little fun?" Sam asked, bending over to put her ankle boots on.

I grunted at the sight of her tight ass. "Well if you ask me, last night was pretty fucking fantastic," The thought of her gifted mouth wrapped around my dick made me hard again.

"Last night was amazing, Oliver, but I meant like going out to Timmy's or Red's Loft. Meet up with some friends, dance and drink, you know?"

I took a step back. "Look, Sam, you know I can't."

"Fine," she huffed. "Call me later. And if I'm not busy, I might come over."

I slammed the door as soon as her foot left the threshold.

I thought things with Sam would have been different. That she would understand that I wasn't ready to be emotionally invested. Taking care of my mother was becoming more and more difficult. I didn't have time nor did I have the desire to invest in something that I knew wouldn't last.

I hated when relationships became complicated.

Actually, I could almost say I hated relationships altogether.

Besides, this was my mom; no one came before her needs. She was my priority and nobody should have expected anything less.

I opened the door to my mother's pale-yellow room. Laney and I had painted it three months ago when the doctor told her that the treatments for her cancer had failed, giving her only a few more months to live. Because she was exhausted and unable to go outside as much as she wanted, Laney and I went to the store and splurged on furnishings, giving her room a full makeover. We imitated the sun and the outside world with white, yellow and soft green colored walls and linen.

As I walked inside, I immediately noticed her smile, which was much different than the previous morning. The day before, she was barely able to talk without wincing in pain. I'd had to administer a lot of morphine compared to her usual dosage, and she ended up sleeping her way through the day into the night.

There were good days and bad ones; it all depended on the medication she had to take to lessen the pain.

"Hey, Mom."

"Good morning, sweetheart. How are you?"

"I'm great. You look like you're in pretty good shape this morning. Did you sleep well?"

Good nights were making themselves scarce. I was always relieved when she woke up well rested.

She nodded. "Did you get into a fight with that girl again?"

"No, Mom. Sam and I are fine." It was pointless to get into *that* conversation with her. "Would you like it if we went outside for breakfast and fresh air?"

She beamed at the idea. My heart would always melt at her enthusiasm for such simple pleasures.

I picked up my mother's small frame, settled her down on the wheelchair beside her bed and covered her body with enough blankets so that she wouldn't get cold. She had lost so much weight since her chemotherapy treatment. It barely took any effort to carry her anymore. It pained me to watch her fade away.

The last time we went to her doctor's office, they informed us that the tumors where spreading faster than anticipated and that she had less than a month to live. That shitty disease was engulfing her whole body. Unfortunately, I had to find a way to accept that, sooner or later, I was going to lose her. There was really nothing left to do other than to wait for the day it would just happen, all the while pretending I was okay and strong enough for the both of us.

I wheeled her out and made my way outside to the gazebo. It was the safest place to be if I wanted to shelter her from the mountain breeze. When I covered her body with the extra blanket, she gave me an annoyed eye roll.

"Oliver, if you put any more blankets on me, I'll die of suffocation. Just go back inside and get me my medication with some tea and a little food to nibble on."

Regrettably, my mother the caffeine junky couldn't drink coffee anymore. Her system was too fragile to digest it. She took the news pretty hard once she found out why she kept having intense heartburn. In fact, she was more crushed by the fact that she couldn't have her caffeine fix, than cancer itself. And even though I suggested quitting along with her she refused. She said that when I drank my coffee while she drank her tea, she could pretend for a couple of sips that it was coffee in her cup not tasteless flower water.

As I made my way back with my coffee and her tea, I stood at the bottom step of our backyard deck and watched my mother's taking in the morning sun and enjoying the beautiful mountain-view. I still had trouble believing this was something we woke up to every morning.

"Here you go, Mom."

"Thank you, honey." Her voice already showed

signs of fatigue.

"Are you cold? Can I get you anything else?" The fact that she was wasting away by the day was eating me up from inside.

"Oliver, just relax. I'm fine." I complied and took a seat beside her. "I think it's time for us to go home, sweetheart."

I waited for her to continue, worried about her sudden memory loss. I hoped there was more to her statement, but she added nothing. I hated when stuff like this happened; I was never really sure how to treat it so she wouldn't take my recovering her mishap too personally. "We are home, Mom."

"No, Oliver, I meant home, like back home. Back to my sister, your father, our family—"

"Mom, Dad's gone. He passed away six years ago," I replied, afraid it might cause her more pain.

She shot me an insulted glare. "I have cancer, Oliver, I'm not suffering from Alzheimer's."

Well that's a relief...

"I'm sorry I offended you. It's just that I thought... you know what? Never mind. I'm sorry."

She let her head fall back to the open sky. "Don't you miss her?" she asked as her gaze tracked a hawk flying nearby. I followed my mother's focus and watched as the predator disappeared between the trees to attacks its next prey.

"Who?"

"Abbygail," she responded blatantly.

As if I was supposed to know whom you're talking about.

My mother's eyes bored into mine and lingered on my uneasy features. I hadn't thought about Abbygail Evens in years. Well that's not quite true. I saw her name on my chest every time I saw my reflection in the mirror, but I refused to put any thought into it.

At least that's what I'd tell myself anyway.

Besides, it had been there for so long, it just felt like it was a part of me. And when girls asked me about it, I would simply find a subtle way to avoid answering them.

I just couldn't understand why my mother would bring this up. "No, I don't."

Her gaze narrowed, and then she sighed.

"What?"

"I don't know. I thought my dying would have at least gotten me a little admission and truth about you and her."

I scratched my jaw and shut my eyes in aggravation. "I don't know what you're talking about. I haven't thought about her in years."

My mother started to laugh, and although it was at my expense, the sound of it was like music to my ears. "Please, Oliver, don't you realize who I am? I'm your mother. I made you. I know you and your heart more than anyone on this planet, especially when it concerns Abbygail Evens. Besides, I can always tell when you're lying to me."

"Whatever, Mom…"

"Do you remember the day you left Carrington?

Yes, a day I would rather forget, thank you very much.

"You told me you and Abby had worked things out the previous night. Guess what, Oliver? I knew it was a lie the second the words came out of your mouth."

"How'd you know that?"

"You scratch your jaw every time you lie," she giggled.

I chuckled. I never realized people noticed I did that. "If you knew it was a lie then why not call me out on it?"

I took a mental note to pay attention to my jaw scratching from that moment on.

"And say what? And what would have been the purpose? You two were too proud to try and talk through it, and in my opinion, you were both smart enough to figure it out on your own."

"You don't know what you're talking about. It had nothing to do with pride."

"Come on, Oliver. Both of you were in love with each other, but wouldn't admit it. If it wasn't pride, then what was it?"

"Fear," I answered without a doubt. "If I admit to loving her then, will you let the subject go?"

"Of course, I won't. Besides, you don't need to

admit to anything because I already knew you were in love with her: your father told me. And let's not forget that you had her name tattooed over your heart at seventeen years old. You don't do that if you aren't in love with someone, Oliver."

"Maybe it was because at that point in my life, I just wanted a reminder of our relationship. Or maybe it was because I valued her friendship more than anything else in this world."

"No. It was because you were in love with her."

I groaned. "Even if I was, which I still refuse to confirm, I haven't thought about her in years. I've dated plenty of girls since I kissed her. As you can see, I am way over Abbygail Evens."

"Please. That's bullshit and you know it. And by the way, thank you for *finally* admitting to kissing her."

I shook my head, annoyed. "I can't believe we're actually talking about this."

"If not now, then when are we supposed to talk about it, Oliver? You know I'm not some girl you're trying to impress. And you definitely don't need to make any excuses to please me like you do with that little brown-haired girl you keep bringing back to my house. I don't really like her by the way."

"God," I complained. "You sound just like Laney."

"Yeah, well, maybe you should start listening to that friend of yours. She knows a lot more than you think. Anyway, this is beside the point. If you are so over Abby, why do you still have so many pictures of her hanging in your room?"

"Because it's my room. I can hang in it whatever I want. Can't I? I like it the way it is—"

"Yet you refuse to sleep in it."

"Fine." I shouted a little too harshly. "I'll take them down if it's what you want. See if I care?"

I do care, a lot. It's the only thing I have left of her.

"It's not what I want, Oliver," she shouted back. "What I want is to go back home. When I die, I want to be buried with your dad, and then, I want you to go knock on the Evens' door and face your fears. I want you to look at Abbygail in the eyes and have the talk you two were supposed to have six years ago."

That's never going to happen...

"Don't roll your eyes at me, young man, and yes, it's going to happen."

Wait. Did I say that out loud? I'm pretty sure I didn't open my mouth...

"You didn't say anything. I can read your face." She pointed a finger at her own. "Mother… remember?"

I released a low snicker.

"Honey, I know she's somewhere down there in your heart and that once in a while she resurfaces in your mind. You refuse to face it because it hurts. You loved her so much, Oliver."

I stood up and leaned on the gazebo fence. I didn't want to talk about this anymore, yet I had no choice but to let my mother say what she needed to say, because I knew I could count on one hand the remaining conversations I would be able to have with her.

"Both of your lives changed the second you left each other's side, and both of you lost a part of your soul along with it. It's time, Oliver. Go home."

I shook my head, denying everything she was saying. But my mom was right and there was no holding back the huge tears of suppressed pain streaming down my face.

How can something that happened so many years ago still affect me like this? It doesn't make any sense.

"Oliver?" My refusal to look at her made her voice soften. "Oliver, I know it's hard, but once you see her, you'll start to heal and unlock your heart."

"Yeah... to pain," I mumbled.

"Maybe, but you may also see that it can unveil much more. Like friendship or affection, desire, passion... love?"

I turned to face her. "Come on, Mom. Love? Six years. Remember?" I shook my head at her delusions. "Six years without seeing her and you think we'll fall back in love?"

"Actually, yes, I do," she admitted. "Oliver, what you two had was different and special. Somewhere deep down, you know I'm right."

"No, I don't. What I know is that you are getting

way ahead of yourself and living in Lala Land. I'm not doing this," I argued, crossing my arms over my chest like a four-year-old. I knew I was being immature, but my mother just couldn't understand how much even this simple conversation was hard for me.

The last thing I wanted was to fight with her, but whenever Abby was concerned, I just couldn't help the feelings creeping up on me.

"Oliver, this is the only thing I ask of you. I just want you to talk to her."

I cursed.

I could tell she was getting impatient with my juvenile attitude. "Don't you think it's time for both of you to at least sit and try to talk? You spent sixteen years of your lives being completely inseparable, for heaven's sake. I'm asking you to try having a simple conversation with her, and you're acting like this is the worst torture ever. SHE WAS YOUR BEST FRIEND."

"You don't understand—"

"YES I DO. You hurt her, and you're still living with the same regret six years later. Tell me, son: if you never face her, how will you ever be able to make things right? How will you ever be able to forgive yourself? How will she ever be able to forgive herself for hurting you?"

Not my problem.

"Mom, the last thing Abbygail said to me was that she hated me. And the last thing she wrote to me, was that she never wanted to see me again. I gave her exactly what she wanted. I stepped out of her life exactly like she wanted me to." I paused, frustrated. "You have no idea what happened between the both of us."

"You think I don't know? I've seen you, I've seen her, and guess what, Oliver? Your Aunt Jenna, is still my best friend. Just because your friendship was destroyed, doesn't me ours was."

Ouch?

"*We* talk... you are the one who doesn't have a clue, Oliver." She suddenly stopped, refraining from saying anything more. I raised my eyebrow curiously, but she folded her arms over her chest, imitating my posture. "Aren't you a little curious to see what she looks like? What she made of herself?" She unfolded her arms and let her anger subside. "Don't you want to know if she's happy?"

"You could tell me. It would make things a lot easier," I joked.

She shook her head. "Listen, Oliver. I can't force you to do this, and I definitely do not want you to do it for me. You need to find the will and desire to do it for yourself. And you know what? Maybe you could also do it for her."

She stayed silent for a minute or so, letting me reflect on everything we'd both said. A cool breeze blew between us, and I figured it was time to take her inside.

"Oliver," she whispered as I put her exhausted body in bed.

"Yeah, Mom?"

"One day, your dad and I will be smiling and watching you both, together again…"

I nodded, pretending to smile. There was no need to provoke another argument with her again. Stepping out, I closed the door ajar and knocked on my old bedroom door to inform Alice, our live-in caretaker, that my mom was asleep and that I would be out for a while.

CHAPTER THIRTY-FIVE

OLIVER

My mom knew I was hurting. Juggling my job, everyday life activities, dealing with her illness and her eventual passing... it wasn't easy. But one night while I was sitting by her bedside talking, she explained that there was something curious about death. She couldn't quite explain the feeling, but she kind of felt relieved that it would soon be over. She'd talk a lot about my dad, and how she couldn't wait to be with him again. It was as if she was at peace with the whole dying thing.

I remember her telling me that she wouldn't leave until she knew I would be ready to let her go, and in the end, it's exactly what she did. Even though her kind soul leaving her body left me devastated, somewhere deep down, I knew that we'd both be okay.

I think this is why my grieving process was a lot less difficult than it was when my father died in that car accident.

As I dialled their number, I started getting nervous. It was late, but my worry was mostly because this was the first time in six years that I had called and not hung up after the first ring. I didn't know much about Abby's life, but my mom had told me that she had moved out of her mom's house years ago.

Even though the likelihood of Abbygail answering the phone at her mother's house was about slim to none, the possibility that I could be hearing Abbygail's voice for the first time in far too long made my heart race and my hands all sweaty.

"Hello?"

Oh, for fuck's sakes, really?

"Uh—"

"Hello?" she repeated.

I shook my head at my fearfulness. "Uh, hi, may I please speak with Mrs. Jenna Evens, please?"

I should have wished her happy birthday.

"Yes, one moment please." I heard muffling then two people talking.

"Who's on the phone?"

"I don't know, but he wants to talk to my mom. Who calls at this time of day anyway?"

It wasn't even that late, like nine thirty or something. I just kept pushing back the phone call until no other family member or friends were left to call.

"Did you check caller ID?"

"Of course, I did. What am I? An idiot? I don't recognize the number."

A small grin spread across my face as I listened to their altercation.

Well, that temper of hers never really changed.

"Mom? Hey Mom," her voice softened, *"I'm so sorry to wake you, but there's some guy on the phone asking for you."*

"Okay, sweetheart, just give me a second. I'll take it. Hello?"

"Um, yes, hi 'Mam," I faltered. "I mean Mrs. Evens, I mean—"

God why is this so awkward?

"Who is this? Do you know what time it is?"

"Yeah, I do. I'm sorry. It's Oliver, Oliver Langton."

"Then it's Aunt Jenna to you, young man."

I winced. Her reaction wasn't one I expected, I didn't deserve to still be considered as her family.

"I'm sorry, Aunt Jen. I know it's late, and I'm sorry I woke you. I'm calling about my mom…" And I went on explaining to my ex-best friend's mother how, as of the previous night, I was officially an orphan.

ABBYGAIL

I listened closely to my mother and as the conversation progressed, there was no mistaking who she was talking to. Standing on the other side of her bedroom door in complete shock, well, not complete shock, I knew the day would end up happening sooner or later; all I wanted was to do was breakdown and cry.

"Okay, Oliver," she sniffed. "Yes, okay. I'll call you tomorrow, sweetheart, and we'll figure something out.

"Yep. Try to get some sleep, and I'll talk to you soon."

I crumbled to the sound of my mother's pained wavering voice. My Aunt Evelyn was gone.

I took out my phone and stared at his number for what seemed like an eternity. Huge teardrops fell over my hands and screen as I debated my next move. Over six years of silence, and there I was still desperate to call the heartless guy that ruined my life by abandoning me.

"Hey, Abs?"

I looked up to Chase and let out a loud relieved sigh. Regardless of what had happened between Oliver and me, one more second and I would have dialed the long-distance number just to make sure he was okay.

"Yeah?"

"Do we need to postpone our movie night?"

I bit the inside of my cheek, trying to retain my own heartache and nodded. "My mother's best friend just passed. If you don't mind I'd like to stay with her tonight."

"Hey." He offered a friendly smile. "Don't worry about it. I completely understand. Tell your mom I'm sorry for her loss, okay?"

"I will. Thank you."

"And Abby," Chase called, going back down the steps. He had been inside our house so often that he didn't need me to show him out. "I'm sorry for your loss, too. I know Evelynn meant a lot."

I watched him turn the corner and slipped my phone back into my pocket. The exhale that escaped me as I stood and walked inside my mother's bedroom was a combination of relief and sorrow.

Memories of my childhood flooded my heart as my mother slept soundly beside me. Restless, I sat up and looked outside her bedroom window. From over our garage, I could clearly see the remainder of the leaves from the willow tree being blown away in any direction the gusty wind would take them.

How I wished my pain could fly away along with them...

Tears ran down my face as I thought about the only

guy I had ever loved. I hated him. Yet there I was wishing I could be over there holding his grieving hand.

Because in truth, that's exactly where I should have been.

CHAPTER THIRTY-SIX

ABBYGAIL

I was asked to testify in court. It was supposed to be a quick thing where I simply related some facts about a case I was involved in with work. The initial plan was to finish work early and go gift shopping for my mother's birthday. Unfortunately, things got hectic at the courthouse, and the case got delayed over and over. It got pushed until the last hearing of the day, and I ended up leaving after five. I spent the whole day waiting in a closed-up eight-by-ten room, with smelly and unsavory company.

Not my idea of a nice day.

Around lunchtime my mother texted me saying that she needed me to pick up some groceries for her, and that she'd be home around five thirty. By the time

I got out of the courthouse, the sun had set, and as our day progressed, so did her extensive list of groceries. Two weeks had gone by since Evelynn's passing, and all my mother did was work. My doing her groceries or running any other of her errands, weren't out of the ordinary, but the fact that she would be getting home before dinner time was a damn miracle.

My brows furrowed as I parked my car in my driveway across the street. I still couldn't believe I was the official owner of my ex-best friend's home. It had all happened so fast... When I turned eighteen my father told me that after deserting us, he started putting money in an account for me. He claimed it was the only way he could manage his guilt over leaving us behind. The plan was that I could use it for whatever I wanted once I became an adult. At first, I refused it. Years of absence couldn't be replaced by a chunk of cash. But then Chase's dad got transferred back to Kingston's military base and the Carter's put Oliver's old house up for sale, so I changed my mind.

Not about my father's presence in my life, but the money: obviously.

During the first few months I alternated between living in my apartment in Ottawa and my new house. It was just easier to skip the traveling time when I went to school. But then life hit me with a load of unplanned bullshit and made me move into my own house, alone, and way earlier than I had planned.

To some of my friends, buying Oliver's childhood house was just plain weird, but to me there was nothing more normal. Even though the Langton's hadn't been a part of my life for years, that household was my second home. I grew up inside its walls, and they were a part of who I was. They reminded me of the person I could be, and every time I stepped inside, I *felt* the calming balm over my unhealed wounds

When I stepped out of my car, my mom's Lexus was nowhere to be seen. She should have been home by the time I'd made it back from the grocery store.

Honestly, I was worried about my mother. Watching her work every possible shift at her dental clinic was driving me nuts. I knew she did it to keep her mind busy, but her overworking herself wasn't healthy. Unfortunately, every time I confronted her about it, her responses were the same: *'My heart is in perfect condition, Abbygail. I can take it.'* Or *'You would do the same if you were in my position, so don't you dare judge me, Abby.'* And the worst part was that she was completely right.

"Mom?" I yelled walking inside her house without knocking.

Well, maybe she is home after all and finally decided to put her garage to use...

"Mom, can you come and give me a hand with

these please?" Knowing very well that she would throw a fit if she heard me walk inside her house with my heels on, I kicked off my pumps. "Mooom?"

"Finally," I mumbled when the bathroom door opened. It was weird that she was using that bathroom and not hers over the garage.

With my hands full, I walked up the three steps towards the kitchen and faced the hallway that lead up to my old bedroom. Ready to request her help again, I opened my mouth to shout, but quickly realized that my mother wasn't the one stepping out. It was a man. And he was just standing there half naked in his lose faded jeans.

I bit down on my lower lip.

The guy was tall, and I couldn't help staring at the impressive art work that covered his well sculpted body. The unbuckled belt of his jeans made them hang low on his hips. As my gaze trailed up and down his frame, unsubtly ogling him, he crossed his arms over his very well-defined abs and smirked.

He was clearly appreciating the look he was getting from me.

Smooth, Abby, real smooth.

I studied him silently. His hand went through his damp, dark brown hair and he licked his lips. When the metallic stud appeared through is sexy grin, I stopped breathing.

His dark stare matched mine. His hand scratched

the scruff of his square jaw, and he stood there, daunting me with his cocky eyes.

Waiting.

It was as if he expected something from me...

Until it happened three seconds later.

Fuck...

NO REGRETS PLAYLIST

You Belong With Me - Taylor Swift
Broken - Seether, Amy Lee
Numb - Linkin Park
Never say Never - The Fray
Demons - Imagine Dragons
Just Give Me a Reason - P!nk (feat. Nate Ruess)
Wildest Dreams - Taylor Swift
Apologize - Timbaland (feat One Republic)
Be The One - The Fray
Say Something - A Great Big World
How's It Going To be - Third Eye Blind
Behind Blue Eyes - Limp Bizkit
Photograph - Ed Sheeran
What Now - Rihanna

ACKNOWLEDGMENTS

I would like to take the opportunity to thank the several people involved in my perseverance throughout the past year.

Danielle, Lise. Thank you for taking a shot at my first draft of No Regrets. Your words gave me the push I needed to push to follow my dream of writing Abby' and Oliver's story.

Patasha... Hell, I wouldn't even know how to thank you. Your help has been beyond what a writer could possibly wish for. From present tense, to ellipsis's... my writing would not be what it is today. I have come a long way and it's because of you. I might have been a good student, but you were the best teachers.

Chelle, from Indie Solutions, I swear to God, I don't know how many times I secretly said you were a pain in my ass. But you were the best pain in the ass ever. Thank you for helping me make this story amazing.

To my editor, cover, teaser designer and formatter, Schmidt Author Services, you've been amazing. Working with you has been a breeze. Thanks for your patience and everything you've done to help with this book.

Kelly, Melissa, Stacey and Colette. Thanks for your support. Thanks for your words of confidence. Thank you for helping me get this book out. Thank you for the hours and hours of your precious time. I have no idea how many times one can say thank you for it to be enough: BUT THANK YOU!!! Without you, I would be completely lost.

Nath, Vicky... Je n'ai aucune idée ce que je ferais sans vous deux. Je vous aime tellement. Merci de tolérer mes folies. Merci d'avoir été aussi présentes. Merci pour votre écoute, vos opinions, vos encouragements, votre support dans ce projet qui me semblait sans fin.

A mon amour et mes enfants, merci pour votre patience. Merci de m'avoir pardonné pour mes oublis. Merci pour vos sourires. Merci de me laisser poursuivre mes rêves, même si parfois il s'agit de vous délaisser pour mes idées et les conversations dans ma tête. Vous êtes ma vie et je vous aime plus que tout au monde.

And to my readers, thank you for your support. I hope you enjoy reading about Abby and Oliver just as much as I loved writing the beginning of their story.

Living with Regrets is available, so go grab it now!

ABOUT THE AUTHOR

Taking care of children is Aimee Noalane's vocation, reading is her passion, and writing is her adventure. She is a wife, mother, foster parent and Canadian author.

Chocolate and candy are her devilish addiction, but if you're really sweet, she might agree to share some with you.

Make sure you join her reader's group @RootBeer Kisses on Facebook.

Stay up to date: www.aimeenoalane.com

Made in United States
North Haven, CT
06 April 2022

17944540R00186